WITCH
UPON A
STAR

CAPRICORN
CURSED

SÈPHERA GIRÓN

For more information contact:
Riverdale Avenue Books
5676 Riverdale Avenue
Riverdale, NY 10471.

www.riverdaleavebooks.com

Design by www.formatting4U.com
Cover by Scott Carpenter

Digital ISBN 9781626012547
Print ISBN 9781626012554

First Edition 2008 published by Ravenous Romance
Second Edition January 2016

A NOTE FROM THE AUTHOR

Welcome to the *Witch Upon a Star* series, where anything can and does happen.

A few years ago, I wrote a couple of books about sexy witches casting spells for romance. These witches belong to a coven, ruled by a High Priestess named Lucy, in a little New England coastal town called Hermana. After I wrote and published the first few books, my real life took a bit of a turn, and so my lovely ladies and the remaining books were put aside for a few years. However, Lori Perkins, who has always championed these witches and this series, gave me a call in the fall and asked me to consider resurrecting my lovely ladies and their magical adventures for her new publishing company, Riverdale Avenue Books.

It wasn't too difficult to persuade me to revisit Hermana and Lucy and the witches. I'm thrilled to be working with Lori on this series, and I can't wait to see what my witches are going to do next!

Part of the fun of working on this series this time around includes the fact that the television shows *American Horror Story, Penny Dreadful, Bates Motel* and *Scream Queens* are hugely popular right now. I love these shows. They have a great knack for telling wild stories with sex, horror and comedy while everyone looks fabulous.

Why does this matter to an erotic writer?

The *Witch Upon a Star* series combines love, lust, horror, passion, comedy and life in much the same way these favorite shows of mine do. People who enjoy watching these shows will understand this series. Even if readers don't watch TV, they will enjoy this series. Each book contains a complete story, a complete roller-coaster ride that follows a birthday girl and her quest for sex and love. A reader can pick up any book and enjoy a lusty magical adventure.

The *Witch Upon a Star* series is set in the fictional New England town, Hermana, Massachusetts that was founded by twin sisters who escaped the Salem witch trials in the 1700's.

The sisters' names were Sorona and Serephena. They both lived well into their 90's, sharing their holistic healing secrets and building up the mystical vibrations of the area. They married twin witches, Nigel and Nathaniel, who shared their voracious sexual appetites and magical healing abilities. Consequently, the foursome enjoyed a long line with many descendants who continued to grow the town and add to its magical and erotic qualities.

The town is rich in tradition and combines the beauty of both ocean and forest. Much like Cassadaga in Florida, Lily Dale in New York, or Sedona in Arizona, Hermana resonates with some sort of vibration that attracts spiritualists, occultists, ghost-hunters, witches and divination experts from all over the world.

The town is about 45 minutes from Boston, a few miles from a major highway, by way of a long, winding road that weaves through a forest, a meadow with a ring of trees, and then into the village. The road leads directly to the ocean, where there is a large, public beach. Some of the residents enjoy nude sunbathing, and in Hermana, anything goes. There are many funky little shops, several pubs, dance clubs, bed and breakfasts, a gym and library. The town is inhabited by people who believe in the power of the sisters and those who do not.

The biggest and most well-known landmark is a huge New England gothic-style house complete with turrets, which is where the sisters originally lived. Of course, it was just a shack when they first cobbled it together in the early founding days, but over the generations, wings, tunnels, wrought-iron fencing and lush gardens were added.

One of their descendants lives there now. Lucy, who is about 80, opens her doors now and again to the town for various celebrations. She has a core group comprised of 12 of the local ladies who meet with her monthly, if not more frequently, to discuss life and love, cast spells and welcome the various equinoxes. Guests are often welcome when there isn't a private ceremony and are allowed to bring questions to the witches.

People flock to Hermana for answers. Some find them. Some do not. Others go for the rumored hedonistic pleasures and usually find something to entertain and entice them.

Each month, the *Witch Upon a Star* series will focus on the romantic quest of a different lady connected to Hermana. January will tell the story of our Capricorn friend, Natasha.

The power of love and lust, magic and mysticism is at the heart of the town, which keeps beating as steadily as the waves that crash along the beach. Connections are made and lost.

Passion ebbs and flows. And still, the town continues to beguile the seekers, the wanderers and the lost to experience its hedonistic pleasures and unearth its darkest secrets.

Welcome to Hermana,

I hope you enjoy your stay.

Welcome to the first book in Witch Upon a Star!

Blessed Be!

Sèphera Girón
January 3, 2016

CAPRICORN

December 22–January 20

Element: Earth

Ruling Planet: Saturn

Symbol: The Goat

Primary Mode: Sensation

Key Phrase: I Master

Life Lesson: We all have to die some day; first live.

Colors: Brown, orange, green, black, gray, indigo, violet

Stones: Diamond—enhances self-confidence, heightens ambition

Falcon's Eye—increases visionary powers, intuition
White Sapphire— promotes discipline

Famous Capricorns: David Bowie, Edgar Allen Poe, Elvis Presley, Pitbull, Betty White, Ellen DeGeneres, Annie Lennox, Patti Smith, Pat Benatar, Michele Obama, Katie Couric, Martin Luther King Jr., Marlene Dietrich, Cary Grant, Henry Miller, Howard Stern, Isaac Asimov, J. D. Salinger, J. R. R. Tolkien, Jack London, Jim Carrey, Janis Joplin, Kid Rock, Marilyn

Manson, Mary Tyler Moore, Mel Gibson, Muhammad Ali, Orlando Bloom, Rod Stewart, Rudyard Kipling, Susan Lucci, Ted Danson, Tia Carrere, Tiger Woods, Victor Borge, Woodrow Wilson

Earth Sign Buzzwords: ambitious, practical, patient, nurturing, stable, reliable, hard-worker, practical, generous, classic, introverted, materialistic, calm, down-to-earth, feminine

Capricorn Traits: Capricorn is represented by the goat that is always climbing to the top of the mountain and the fish that is intuitive. Capricorns can be dreamers with a mission, and they often get their tasks completed. Capricorns are known for having the driest wit in the zodiac. Sometimes people just don't get them. They are careful-minded people also known for their pessimism. They consider facts judiciously before taking action. They aren't afraid of hard work, which is a good thing since they can be materialistic and house-proud. Capricorns are rather secretive and shy. They are sensitive and have a fear of rejection, although they can be rather egotistical about their talents as well. Capricorns are horny goats whose sexual desires are often bubbling just below the surface.

Natasha's forecast:
Secrets are prominent and hold the key to an auspicious future. Listen to the messages that others are trying to tell you. Follow your instincts and go with your gut feelings. A mysterious stranger holds your fate in his hands. Don't be so reticent with your emotions.

Chapter One

A new year brings new beginnings.

Plant Killer

It was a sunny day, which was rare during the gloomy New England winters. Rarer still was Natasha being awake on such a day. In fact, she had stayed up so late that it was nearly noon, long past her bedtime.

Natasha blocked out the light by drawing the heavy, velvet, burgundy curtains shut. She turned back to the living room, searching for any stray ray that may have slipped through the cracks. The flickering flames from several tall, tapered candles in wrought-iron candelabras now cast the only light. She returned to her plush velvet couch and goblet of cranberry juice to relax with her book.

Anyone looking in at her would see a tall, lanky woman with a long, pale face, a dark, penetrating stare and waist-length, black hair who was half-lying on the plush pillows. Natasha turned the pages of her book with long, delicate fingers and studied the words with intensity. But this was a facade; no one could really see the *real* Natasha.

1

The espionage novel she was reading wasn't catching her interest. Soon she was restlessly looking around the room. Tall piles of books teetering on wooden tables surrounding her. Hundreds more lined the heavy wooden shelves that sprawled along the walls. The room was large enough to house both her living room and dining room. A claw-foot wooden table held a bouquet of fake black roses and lace doilies on a black tablecloth. Although she hadn't had anyone over for dinner in months, she was always ready in case the opportunity arose.

Her mind drifted lazily to New Year's Eve with Gus. They had slipped away to one of the bedrooms to talk quietly, away from the raucous party. His voice was low and deep, soothing her in the darkness. His hand had cupped the curve of her face when he first pressed his lips against hers; his breath was hot and tasted of champagne. Hunger swelled in her, a hunger for more of his taste.

The kiss had been short and tentative. When he pulled back, she leaned into him, kissing him again. Their kisses grew deeper and longer, her tongue rooted out his. They fell onto the bed together.

How secure she had felt with his arms wrapped around her. His scent was still in her nostrils as she remembered the heady aroma of his cologne mixed with sweat. His broad, muscular chest was firm against hers as they rolled around in one of Lucy's private rooms. His lips had eagerly sought hers out as if he were as hungry for affection as she was. Their hands had roamed along each other's bodies, pressing and pulling at unfamiliar flesh. Their urgency had grown through their kisses, and their half-clothed bodies

2

tangled around each other. As she considered whether she should unbutton his pants, the moment was suddenly over.

Someone burst into the room looking for coats, interrupting them long before anything meaningful could happen. The interruption had rendered them shy once more.

It was nearly dawn when Lucy's New Year's party broke up. Natasha had noticed the red fingers of the sun climbing up the horizon and realized it was time to leave. She had to leave. There was really no choice in the matter. Gus had gone off to socialize with friends once they returned from the bedroom, and though she glanced through the crowd, she hadn't noticed where he had ended up. Many of the party guests used the impending dawn as a reason to call it a night, a day, a year.

In the rush of people, Natasha never had a chance to say good-bye to him as she grabbed her violin case and set out for home.

She wondered if she would see him again. She wondered if he wanted to see her again.

Natasha hadn't noticed him around town before, but Hermana was rather large. Since she didn't go out much during the day, she didn't know if he could have been living and working here for years. Men came and went. Some were special. Some, not so much. Such was the way of life.

Again she attempted to focus on the words in front of her, but they lazily swam away. The idea of spies blasting each other from hidden places just wasn't holding her attention, as dreamy romantic ideas flitted around her tired mind.

Looking around the room, she was aware of all the

darkness—black candelabras, black lamps, black table dressings, even black books. Normally, she enjoyed all the blacks and burgundies that furnished her space, but as ideas of romance circled her thoughts, she wondered if all the dark colors were just a black hole where her emotions hid.

She yearned for some greenery in the dimness, but whenever she brought home a new plant, it died. The only current survivor was a three-foot tree in the corner, but even that wasn't faring too well.

She went to the kitchen to fill her copper pot with water from the cooler. The shiny metal glimmered in the darkness. The running water reminded her of the first time she laid eyes on the pot. It had been in the hands of Countess Lydia (of some small European town she would have to look up again in her diary) as she showed Natasha the proper way to water plants. Even as Natasha stood beside the beautiful countess, the brilliant green leaves around her turned a dull yellow as they slowly shriveled and died.

The countess had turned to her with a gleam in her eye.

"As I expected, you are one of them." The countess studied her as she questioned Natasha. "How can I show you to care for plants when you are destruction?"

Natasha shivered as she remembered the look of betrayal in the countess's eyes. No matter how much she forgot over the years, the hurt in that she had seen in those eyes never left her heart.

The pot was nearly full, and Natasha turned off the tap. As she walked toward the small tree, a Malabar chestnut, in the corner of the living room, its leaves fluttered lightly.

"Now, now, I'm just trying to feed you."

As she approached the plant, it turned a light yellow and tightly curled up its leaves. Natasha sighed and stepped back. The tree uncurled hesitantly the farther away she went.

"Two days old and already you're leaving me. So much for my money *feng shui*." She returned to the kitchen and poured the water down the drain. Sighing, she went over to her computer and flicked it on. She checked her email. Nothing except her daily horoscopes.

"A new year brings new hope."

Natasha sighed. Didn't beginning-of-the-year horoscopes always say that?

She noted that the full moon was on her birthday, and she considered that rather auspicious. The moon was going from Cancer to Leo, so she imagined she would have some vivid dreams and lusty thoughts.

Finally, sleep beckoned her. She returned to the living room to snuff out her candles. She stopped at the small altar set up by the window.

There were a few simple tokens on it, and she touched each one lightly. "Thank you for your blessings."

She went into her bedroom, where a huge king-sized bed with a thick burgundy velvet canopy loomed. The bed was the centerpiece of the room, but it still didn't detract from the ornate matching dresser and highboy. There was also a wardrobe. But, her favorite item, one she had kept for years, was her vanity table.

The little claw-footed, mirrored dresser had once belonged to someone. She couldn't quite remember

5

who and knew she would have to refer to her diary again. There was the vague idea that it had been payment, likely for music classes. The matching stool was upholstered with burgundy velvet. Although it was worn, it was still a beautiful piece.

Once a week, Natasha wandered around her rooms with lemon oil and cloths, shining up her precious wooden pieces until they gleamed like the moon on the beach at low tide.

She put on her favorite white cotton nightgown with the ruffled sleeves and slipped into bed. Lost among the pillows and comforters, she reached out to tie the canopy flaps shut. With a black-silk-and-lace mask over her eyes, she smiled as she tried to sleep, willing herself toward thoughts of Gus once more.

In minutes, she came to her.

"Not tonight," Natasha whispered. "I'm tired."

The spirit was persistent, teasing her face with ethereal, floating fingers. Natasha batted at her with her hand.

"No. I don't want to know."

Natasha rolled over, turning her back to the ghost, but it was to no avail. The ghost teased her mask from her face, forcing Natasha to look at her.

The ghostly presence shimmered in the darkness, a full mouth and wide, expectant eyes flitted in and out of Natasha's focus. Another form shifted into shape next to the ghost and then another one. Soon, lost souls crying to Natasha for attention filled the canopy tent.

"Go away," she said firmly to them as she sat up. "I don't want to see you right now." Slowly, the images faded, and Natasha flopped back onto her pillows.

Curse this so-called gift! Why is there always a price?

Her dreams were no better, which was not surprising. The stronger her *gift* of speaking to the dead grew, the more she was unable to control it. Between unexpected messages from beyond and her constant thirst, she was going mad.

By the time she awoke, she was dizzy and weak. She opened up the great velvet drapes and greeted the night. It was chilly in the room; she could almost see her breath. She knew it had nothing to do with the snowstorm outside. It was the ghosts, lurking in wait for her to answer their questions and relay messages to their loved ones.

Her fingers itched as she prepared the coffeemaker. Once it was percolating, she went into the living room. There was a bit of a glow from the moon as the whiteness of the pounding snow swirled outside her windows.

Natasha loved her loft. It sprawled across the entire floor of an old factory from the '20's. Some company had once thought Hermana might be a good trade town. If there had been more workers able to focus on toiling in a factory, it would have been.

With Boston and other towns not that far away, the Hermana textiles factory didn't fare well. It may also have had something to do with the local citizens not being terribly excited about a big, black-smoke-belching factory smack-dab in the middle of their little scenic town.

It could also have been the witches.

There had been a series of unfortunate events, which included missed shipments and faulty machinery. There had even been that horrible day when the nasty, old foreman fell into some spinning thing and was sliced and diced beyond recognition.

No matter, the factory was abandoned within years of being built. It was eventually converted into large, beautiful lofts for artists and other eccentrics.

Although her living room and dining room area were combined, there was lots of room for any number of guests that a single lady might expect to have over. There was her bedroom, which was lovely, but her other room was her total pride and joy—the room where her angry soul found peace. In it, she could lose herself for hours from the sheer exhaustion of living; she could be single and alone, with no family and no destination.

The room called to her—sometimes invading her dreams, sometimes niggling at her when she was out with friends. She had spent countless hours saging the room, ridding it of the angry workers and the wailing foreman who were drawn to her.

It was the only room where she was able to somewhat hide from the spirits, but even then, it was seldom for long.

She turned the large goat's head handle and pushed the door open.

She flicked one of the many switches, and several huge wrought-iron chandeliers with electric candles burst into life. The room was covered with thick red carpet, not only across the floor but also along the walls and across the ceiling. There was another door leading to the back staircase, which was covered in black carpet so it was easy to locate.

The room had giant speakers, an area with a drum

kit and several microphone stands. There was another area with one music stand and a ceiling-high bookcase stuffed full of music books and papers. Recording equipment, wires, microphones and boxes of CDs were on the shelves. To Natasha, there was nothing more important in life than vibrating with music. It didn't matter if it was booming from speakers at a club or quivering beneath her fingers on her violin strings.

There were several instrument cases, and Natasha went over to one of the violins. She opened up the case and pulled out a bow. She examined it for warps as she tightened it and then slid rosin along it. She lifted out the violin and fastened the shoulder rest. As she put it to her shoulder, she picked up her bow again. She trembled with excitement as the bow easily slid along the strings. A warm, rich sound enveloped the room as she played, fingers dancing easily along the fingerboard.

An hour passed before she remembered her coffee. She put away her violin and snapped off the lights. With a sigh, she shut the music room door behind her and returned to reality.

After sipping several cups of coffee and checking her email, she began to feel like herself, almost. There was still that gnawing, unending hunger in her belly, but she pushed it aside. It wasn't time yet. She had to wait to quell her appetite.

It was part of her Capricorn self-discipline. Waiting. Self-restraint, patience and anticipation of the perfect moment.

She was going to meet Ellie and Maggie for drinks at Intuition, and she still had to bathe and apply her face.

Around her, the room swelled with the nudging of impatient spirits, but she told them to leave her alone as she entered the bathroom.

The steam from the shower filled her with a sense of longing. For a moment, she caught a glimpse of herself under a waterfall in South America with Paolo, a coffee bean farmer. He had been darkly tanned, muscular and rather tall. His thick accent and strong worker hands had attracted her to him. During her time in his village, they had spent many hours together enjoying each other's bodies.

The afternoon in the waterfall was a memory she would cherish forever. She had written it down and revisited it regularly so she wouldn't forget it.

His lips had searched hers out so eagerly as she pressed into him. She was still young then, still able to handle the sun when she kept her eyes squinted shut. His hands had eagerly cupped her breasts as she arched into him with a moan.

His body had pressed tightly against hers, and she felt the firm swell of his cock against her stomach.

"I want to make love to you," he had whispered hotly into her ear.

She nuzzled into him. "Yes, yes."

He slid into her, his body tight and strong as he held her under the soothing, steady stream of the waterfall. She knew he could do whatever he wanted to her and she could never get sick or pregnant. Not her kind.

He held her, pushing into her urgently, grabbing fistfuls of her long, dark hair.

"I want to try something else," he said as he pulled out. They waded to the rocky wall of the cave, and he moved her so she stood facing it, her hands clutching the damp rocks for support as he slipped into her again. His cock was rigid and parted her flesh easily. She gasped as the different angle activated new sensations. His hands pulled her hips back to push against him as he thrust into her. The wall was slippery, and her hands slid along it as she tried to balance. The delicious prodding of his urgency melted with her own, and she threw her head back.

Their feet slipped on the rocks, and the rushing water threw them off balance, so he took her by the hand to the grassy shore to finish.

She lay on her back on the soft grass as he pushed her legs over her shoulders. Again, he entered her, and she gasped as he seemed even bigger than before. She held onto his broad shoulders as his breath panted hot against her neck. She let pleasure course through her, as he whispered Spanish words into her ears.

In the shower, Natasha's soapy fingers worked her clit as she imagined Paolo fucking her that day. As she closed her eyes, fingers stroked her along her shoulders and back. Warm, soapy caresses warmed her round bottom. Her own hand found her breast, and she toyed with the nipple as she tingled and moaned. Another hand fondled her hair, and she squeezed her eyes tighter, not wanting to see the apparitions who were touching her.

At last, she came, just as the hot water was running low. She opened her eyes as the shower curtain fluttered, then stilled. The door to the bathroom clicked shut, and she shook her head.

Who are they kidding?

She rinsed off the soap and stepped out of the tub, feeling less tense and more ready to face her friends. She

11

returned to her bedroom with one large, white bath towel firmly wrapped around her body while another donned her head turban-style. The warm steam from the bathroom wafted in, and it was welcome in the chilly room.

She caught a glimpse at herself in the mirror. Contrary to legend, she could see her reflection quite fine. She could see all sorts of things in mirrors. She was paid well for her skill.

Tonight, there was only her face staring back. A very young face, stern and cold, but a pretty face nonetheless.

It wasn't a trick.

Back when she had first heard about it, she didn't believe it. However, in her decades of living, she was proud she had followed the advice, as despicable as it seemed. When she looked in the mirror, she saw a woman in her 30's. Tall, slender, and pale. Just like the others that had turned her.

Marianne had told her the secret.

Marianne.

She remembered Marianne because she had painstakingly handwritten her story in one of the leather-bound journals on the bookcases in her living room. She read the journal often to remind herself who she really was and how to continue on. In fact, she stopped her preparations to go into the library to retrieve the journal.

She had to keep rereading her past, and since she was thinking about Marianne, she thought she'd better read about her quickly.

There was a whole thick journal dedicated to Marianne. Natasha opened the book and relived their first encounter.

Chapter Two

When two souls collide, listen.

Marianne

When Marianne first appeared to her, it was as if in a dream. Natasha was having a pint of beer at one of the pubs on a dreary New England night.

That was nearly two hundred years ago, when Hermana was still a child turning adolescent. Unescorted women were frowned upon in pubs in regular towns, but not in this town. Women were treated the same, if not better, than men. Natasha was still new to the area, but she had grown rather attached to a pub called The Kettle. Centuries later, during the New Age 90's, the name was changed to Intuition.

That night, though, the pub was still The Kettle and Natasha sat nursing a pint of dark beer, staring morosely at the world around her. The bar wasn't very crowded, and most of the regulars were watching a blue-eyed young man playing a recorder at the far end of the room.

Natasha could tell by sly glances and the movement of lips that a few people were whispering about her.

They could have been gossiping about any number of things. Natasha didn't care. A great melancholy had seized her, and she hoped to drown it in beer.

The clock chimed midnight, and the door blew open. A tiny, blonde woman burst into the room with a gust of wind and leaves, her shawl wrapped tightly around her. The lady scurried in, soaked to the bone. She headed for the bar and plunked herself down on a high wooden stool.

Natasha watched as the woman ordered a beer, and then she looked quickly around the bar before pulling out a dog-eared, rain-soaked, leather-bound book. The woman shivered as she drank her beer, frozen fingers trying to flip the pages of the little book that had a big pentacle on the front.

The woman was startled as Natasha stood beside her.

"You're all wet," Natasha said. Her attraction to the woman mystified even herself. She didn't know why she was standing beside her, nor did she know why she was so curious about that little leather-bound book.

"Pretty bad out there."

"Here, take off that shawl and put this one on for now. Better yet, come join me at my table."

A buzzing sensation raced through Natasha's fingers as she helped the stranger off with her shawl and wrapped her in Natasha's own. This woman was something more than she seemed. Tiny, frail, pale, but strong. A sickness formed in the pit of Natasha's stomach. The smell. She was death.

She's like me.

"Thank you," the woman said as she tossed her

golden curls. Her dark brown eyes were like patches of coal. Natasha's own dark eyes burned into the woman's as she held out her hand.

"Natasha," she said. "Marianne."

They stared each other, sisters of the skin but afraid to say it aloud. Their observations were broken by the bartender.

"Pretty bad out still, huh?" the bartender asked.

Marianne nodded.

"It's coming down hard. But it's not that cold. Really." Marianne shivered, rubbing her hands along her faded blue blouse. Natasha noted with interest that as old as the blouse may have been, the handiwork on it was remarkable. Marianne gave the bartender a few coins.

"Thank you," the server said. "Keep warm. Stay as long as you like, Marianne. You know that."

"Yes, I do, Elsie." Elsie returned to her station at the bar. Natasha and Marianne stared into their beer.

"Where did you get that blouse?" Natasha finally asked, looking up at Marianne. "England. I brought it with me when I came over. I used to have all kinds of fine clothes. But I have no one to send me anything anymore." She sighed.

"Oh, that's a shame. It's very fine work." Natasha touched the stitching on the hem. The sewing was very neat and very strong.

"I had a tailor, once upon a time," Marianne said. She nervously fingered her book. Natasha looked at it.

"What are you reading?" Natasha asked.

"This is a collection. Of spells."

"Whose?"

"A collection." Marianne sighed. "Some are mine. Some I've gathered from others over the years."

"What kind of spells?"

"All sorts. It's really quite fascinating."

"Do any of them work?"

Marianne smiled.

Natasha nodded and looked around. They were getting stares. The whispering was ongoing, and the shushing noises were getting on Natasha's nerves.

"Do you want to go somewhere else?" Natasha asked. Marianne nodded as she finished her beer.

"Definitely."

The rain was still coming down full force. Natasha took Marianne's hand and pulled her along the cobblestone sidewalk.

"Come with me. I'm not far."

They made their way up to the loft Natasha lived in at the time. That place had long been bulldozed and renovated into a library in the 50's.

Natasha showed Marianne the washing-up room and gave her a night robe. As Natasha sat at her vanity and brushed her long, dark hair, she stared with worry at her own face. Deep crevices were forming around her eyes and mouth. She frowned, the lines growing deeper.

Marianne returned, a vision of loveliness in white cotton, her long, curly, blond hair framing her pale, cherubic face. Again, the nausea returned to Natasha as she stared at the beautiful creature before her.

"What's wrong?" Marianne asked.

"I'm sorry. You're so beautiful," Natasha said. "Thank you." Marianne giggled. "I have a secret.

"Eternal youth?" Natasha laughed.

"No, silly girl. I came here to share it with you."

Marianna leaned over to kiss Natasha, who pushed her back.

16

"Don't."

Marianne stared at Natasha, her lower lip pushed out in a pout.

"Don't you like me? I know you do. I can see it in your beautiful, dark eyes."

"It's not that. It's…what you are."

"I am what you are."

"I…know. Why are you here? Who sent you?"

Marianna sighed. She flounced onto the bed and looked up at Natasha. "If you must know, it was your Aunt Lydia. She's worried that you're going to age too fast. She's busy with some work, so she sent me to show you."

Natasha stared at the creature on the bed. She stood up and walked slowly toward her. "How do you know Aunt Lydia?"

"Does it really matter? We go way back."

"No, I don't suppose it does. So show me." Natasha sat beside her.

"In due time. We have to wait for tomorrow, when the stars are in perfect alignment. Then I'll show you what to do."

Marianne touched Natasha's cheek with her soft, long fingers. "In the meantime, you are very beautiful."

Marianne leaned forward to kiss her. Her mouth breathed forth a foul odor reminiscent of moldy leaves, damp moss, and stale beer rotting in the bottom of a mug for a week. Natasha tried to ignore the smell as she pursed her lips. As Marianne drew closer, Natasha turned away once more.

"We will wait for tomorrow. I want to know this secret," Natasha said as she stood and went over to her dresser. She sprayed a small dash of cologne onto a handkerchief and held it to her nose. She breathed in the fresh rose-water scent, and the nausea passed.

"Tomorrow, then."

Natasha left Marianne to the bed and sprawled across her chaise lounge. She didn't sleep a wink all night, and she didn't think Marianne did either.

The next evening, after they awoke and nibbled on bread and cheese, they left the loft. The rain had stopped at some point during the day, and the muggy New England heat created patches of fog along the cobblestone roads.

There were many half-finished houses along the roads as building was ongoing. Many of the roads were, in fact, still cow paths and horse trails, winding through the growing city.

The streets were busy with people returning home from work or heading out for a night at one of the pubs. Hermana back then was a town comprised of many types of outcasts. The sisters who had founded it decades earlier were believed to be witches, but with the new witch town came tricksters and magicians of all kinds. Natasha had come because of her curse and her love of music. She had taken to playing many types of instruments over the years and had heard Hermana allowed women to play in public.

Natasha had become known for her mournful violin tones. Whether she was standing on the street corner or in a garden, many people had given her money to serenade them. She had played at weddings and at other celebrations. Her musical reputation had followed her from Boston. Her other reputation was still a secret only known to a few, such as Marianne.

Marianne led her from the main cobblestone streets toward the large, white, wooden schoolhouse. Most of the local children attended the multi-roomed school, but in the evenings, older people gathered there to discuss books or teach each other math and other concepts. The idea of the school housing different activities for different ages was rather cutting-edge for the time.

Natasha had heard that sometimes-select people during late night sessions even discussed the subjects that had begun the hysteria.

"Why are we here?" Natasha asked as Marianne led her around the building to the back gardens.

"There are two girls who come here almost every night. We need to entice them back to your place."

"To feed?"

"Better." Marianne's eyes lit up, but her lips remain closed.

Natasha didn't question her again.

The women wandered through the gardens and then sat on a stone bench that was nearly hidden under a tall lilac bush. They sat quietly and listened to the crickets chirping and the odd chatter from people walking down the distant street.

As Marianne predicted, two young ladies quietly entered the backyard. Their long dresses swished in the stillness of the night as giggles escaped their lips. They scurried through the garden, knowing the way easily in the darkness, and settled on one of the other benches that was farther down the garden from Natasha and Marianne. Natasha noted with astonishment that the ladies hadn't seen them sitting under the lilac bush.

The young ladies' voices echoed around the garden as they discussed the young men who made their hearts sing. Their voices grew louder as the darkness made them brave. Their musings reminded Natasha of what it was like to be young and innocent.

Once upon a time, she had been young and innocent. She was certain of it. Marianne found Natasha's hand in the darkness and squeezed it.

The girls discussed how they could get the boys to notice them, their naive questions about more intimate matters bringing a smile to Natasha's lips. She deduced that the dark-haired girl was Misty and the fairer girl was Samantha.

As the girls prattled on, Marianne stood up, pulling Natasha with her. She approached the girls, who were startled at her presence.

"It's rather late for proper young ladies to be out," Marianne said sternly. The girls instantly stood, bowing their heads in submission.

"We're sorry. We lost track of time," said Misty.

"You can see that it is dark. Don't you know bad things can happen to you in the darkness?" Marianne asked.

"We know. We're sorry. We'll be going home now," Misty said. She took Samantha's hand, and they turned to go.

"Wait," Marianne said. "I didn't mean to scare you. Why don't we take you somewhere safe? I live not far from here."

Natasha stared at Marianne. Her body was stiff and her eyes were penetrating as she fixed her gaze on Misty's. Natasha wondered what Marianne had in mind.

"Show us," Misty said.

Marianne led the girls silently back to Natasha's home. Natasha didn't say a word as they made their way back down the dark, damp streets.

Once they were in the loft, Marianne smiled. It was more like a cold grimace and didn't quite reach her eyes.

"Why don't you ladies relax and tell us about yourselves?" she said. "In fact, I'll leave Natasha here with you while I go prepare something to drink."

Natasha stared blankly at the girls seated on her chaise lounge as they stared worriedly back at her.

"Don't worry," Natasha said. "Marianne is a nice woman."

"You have such an interesting accent," Misty said. "Where are you from?"

"Many places. It doesn't matter anymore," Natasha said. "For now, I'm from here."

Marianne returned with four goblets of a dark liquid. She handed one to each of the women. As she sat, she lifted her own glass.

"To new friends." Marianne grinned. The girls lifted their glasses. "Now drink. Enjoy. Tell us about yourselves," she coaxed.

Misty sipped her drink and made a face. "Oh, this is bitter."

"It takes a sophisticated palate to really enjoy it," Marianne teased.

Samantha tasted hers and tried not to make a face. "It's rather nice, really," she said as she tried more. She shuddered but continued to drink nonetheless.

Natasha sampled her drink with curiosity, and to her delight discovered it was her favorite berry juice.

She looked over at Marianne and raised an eyebrow. Marianne pretended not to notice as she continued to talk to the girls.

"So, are you ladies engaged?"

They both giggled, faces flushed as they instinctively took more sips of the bitter brew. "I wish," Misty said. "But my fellow doesn't even know I'm alive."

"Neither does mine," Samantha lamented.

"Oh, that's too bad." Marianne crossed the room and peered out the window at the moon. It was high in the sky with puffs of gray fog hugging it. "I imagine neither of you have ever been engaged before."

The idea of it brought peals of laughter from the girls. "Mercy, no," Misty said. "I've never even kissed a boy."

"Me, neither."

Marianne turned back to look at them.

"Aren't you rather old to have never kissed a boy?" Marianne asked Samantha.

"I don't know. I'm a good girl. I'm waiting to kiss on my wedding day."

"I see." Marianne raised an eyebrow, her long, white teeth glinting out from her narrow lips. "Your wedding day. That could be such a long time."

"I can wait. I don't see what the big deal is," Samantha said stubbornly.

"Me, neither," Misty said as she took a long sip as if to prove it.

"Kissing can be so lovely," Marianne said. "Once you've tried it, you'll wonder why you never did it."

"That's what I'm afraid of. What if once I start kissing, I don't want to do anything else?" said Misty.

"You really shouldn't worry your pretty little head about such foolishness. Kissing

should be done by everyone to everyone as often as possible. It's an energy exchange."

"Energy exchange? Like in Wicca?"

"Something like that," Marianne said. "Surely your mothers have taught you that the giving and receiving of external energy will make you stronger and more powerful."

"I've heard my mother speak of such things," Samantha said. "She also warned that it's dangerous and to wait until I'm married."

"It's so like a mother to deprive her daughter of life's greatest pleasures," Marianne retorted.

"My mother wants what's best for me," Samantha said.

"She's jealous of your youth. Your beauty." Marianne sat between Samantha and Misty on the chaise lounge. She draped her arms around the girls, her fingers lightly touching the swell of their breasts.

"No. My mother is still beautiful. I won't believe she's jealous of me," said Samantha

"You are still young. A virgin. You don't know how women really are. You won't fully understand their secrets until you have your first kiss."

"How would a kiss change who I am?" Misty asked. "I don't believe you. "A kiss changes everything. Why else are you waiting for marriage?"

The girls nodded as they drained their glasses. Marianne grinned and Natasha shivered. The smell from Marianne was growing stronger, and Natasha stood up to open a window. The room was stifling hot, and sweat stains were beginning to form under everyone's armpits.

Marianne stood and gathered up the girls' glasses. Before they could protest, she had returned with full glasses.

"Drink. Tell us your thoughts," she said softly.

"I want to kiss," Misty said. "I want to see how it can change things." Her face grew red. "Maybe I shouldn't have said that. I just feel like I want to kiss."

"It's okay." Marianne sat back down between the girls. She stroked Misty's leg. "It's normal to want to kiss. It's what keeps the world going around."

"I want to kiss, badly. Now," Misty said. She leaned clumsily into Marianne and kissed her. As she pulled away, Marianne pulled her back.

"No, like this." Marianne pressed her lips against Misty's, slowly and sensuously. Misty leaned into her, eagerly meeting her lips. Natasha watched with interest while Samantha sipped more of her drink.

At last, Marianne pulled away. Misty grinned and looked around the room. She reached for her glass.

"What was it like? Are you wiser now?" Samantha asked.

Misty looked at the older women and shrugged. "I feel the same. But good. And since I didn't kiss a man, it doesn't count."

"No, it's practice," Natasha said. "Like when you play an instrument."

"I want to try," Samantha said. "Kiss me."

Marianne kissed Samantha with the same intensity she had kissed Misty. Natasha watched and sipped her juice. When the kiss was broken, Samantha leaned back.

"That was splendid." Samantha sighed. As she sank into the softness of the couch, she closed her

24

eyes. Within seconds, she was snoring. Misty stared at her friend.

"She's asleep," she said. "Samantha, wake up."

Misty shook Samantha, but the girl continued to snore lightly.

"What's wrong with her? What did you do?" Misty's eyes grew wide as she watched Marianne stand up and pace across the room.

"I did nothing. She's just asleep. Much like you will be soon," Marianne said firmly. "I'm not going to sleep. You've bewitched us," Misty said. She tried to stand but fell back on her sleeping friend. "Oh my goodness, I can't move my legs."

"Don't fight, just sleep," Marianne said firmly as she continued to stare out the window. At last, Misty's protests stopped and she too was deep in sleep.

"Finally," Marianne said.

Natasha looked at the sleeping girls. "Now what?"

"Now it begins."

"It" was a slow process to which Natasha became addicted over the years. The actual acquiring of the virgin blood was a much messier job than feeding, but the results were well worth it.

* * *

"This is the hardest part. But, it's worth it. Trust me." They had drowned the girls in a tub of water, and Marianne had slit their flesh to allow blood to mix with the water.

"I'm so hungry," Natasha whined.

"It's not for food, Natasha. You must wait and see."

Natasha stared at the wasted blood, licking her lips as her stomach grumbled. Marianne left the washing-up room and went into the living room. Natasha took the moment alone to scoop up some of the blood with her hand and bring it to her mouth.

The warm, salty taste danced on her tongue. Her stomach rumbled louder, craving more and more. She didn't dare take more than a handful. Then another handful while she heard Marianne bustling in the other room. She didn't know what Marianne had in mind, but she was hungry. Very hungry. A little taste wouldn't ruin whatever spell it was they were supposed to be doing, she hoped.

Marianne returned carrying an old pickle bottle of herbs and her well-worn book of spells. She looked at Natasha's blood-smeared face.

"Couldn't wait, could you?" she joked. "Like a little kid staring at candy."

"I'm hungry, Marianne. I don't know how to control myself yet. I don't know how to get through a day, a week, without the constant, aching craving."

"Darling, you'll never get over the craving. Some of us learn self-denial for self-preservation, but others are careless, feasting whenever they want. They're usually the ones who end up with a stake in their heart."

"I didn't ruin the spell, did I?" Marianne laughed. "No, not at all. You can even have a tiny bit more before we start."

Naked, Natasha leaned back into the bathtub and pulled Misty's body so she was sitting up more. Natasha bit into the soft, meaty flesh of her neck and enjoyed another taste of the waning, warm blood. She moaned with

26

pleasure, keeping one eye on Marianne until she waved her hand.

"Okay, that's enough. Get me some candles," Marianne said as she thumbed through her book.

Natasha brought back several candles, not certain what colors might be required. After some thought, Marianne picked five candles and arranged them around the bathtub. As she lit them, she spoke foreign words from her book.

The candles flickered, casting eerie shadows around the room. Marianne's face was harsh in the gloom as she sprinkled herbs into the tub.

Her voice droned and the candles glowed. Natasha was almost hypnotized by the time Marianne stopped. The sight of all the blood made her giddy, and she was glad she'd been allowed a little taste.

"That's it," Marianne said, her girlish demeanor returning. "Really? And what is 'it'?"

"Oh, you'll see. I want it to be a surprise. But you must wait another day. The planets have to shift once more. Come, let's go to bed."

"But I'm not tired. I have two dead girls in my bathtub. And I'm hungry."

"We will remove them tomorrow. In the meantime, we must wait one full day. Otherwise it won't work. We have to follow the transits. I have charts that I'll give you once you understand."

Natasha spent another fitful night on the chaise lounge, half watching Marianne, half pondering the girls in her bathtub. The smell of their raw blood excited her, and she wondered how Marianne had been able to be so calm and collected. Perhaps Marianne had fed recently so she wasn't as crazed as Natasha.

The next night, Marianne showed her a dark secret.

They lit candles, said some words, and danced in the incense smoke.

They dragged the girls from the bathtub and rolled them up in heavy carpets they had retrieved from the dump.

Bloodstained water with herbs and spices still filled Natasha's tub. They added a few more buckets of hot water. Marianne piled several pieces of cloth near the tub as well as two large goblets.

"Remove your clothes," Marianne said as she unlaced her shirt. When both women were naked, Marianne held her hand. "You will never forget this day, this night. You will never forget me. For this is the secret of your existence and the soul of your expectations."

Marianne nodded to the bathtub. "You may go first."

"In there?" Natasha said.

"Yes, the time is right. The planets are aligned. Our Venus, our moon, our Neptune all conjoin to bring us our deepest desires. And what woman doesn't desire eternal youth?"

Natasha stepped into the warm water and sat down. Marianne slid in on the opposite side. They hooked their legs around each other to keep from slipping.

Marianne took one of the many cloths and rubbed it along Natasha's body. Natasha enjoyed the sensation of the bloody water along her body. She took a cloth and washed Marianne. They scooped the herb-soaked, watery blood into the large goblets. They toasted to eternal youth as they drank the potion. Natasha had never tasted such a delicious, salty-sweet flavor in all her life.

As she drank, a new energy coursed through her. The gift of youth swelled through her veins, causing her wrinkles to plump back to fresh-faced flesh and her frown to evolve into a smile. She felt as though she could walk to Boston and back in the snow and not have to catch her breath once.

They lay in the bathtub, sipping their drinks and thinking their own random thoughts. Natasha's mind was still and calm for the first time in ages.

After several hours, Marianne indicated the larger cloths by the tub. "We should get out, and we should try not to mess up your washing-up room too much," she said.

They helped each other out of the tub, rubbing their bodies with the scraps of material, trying to keep the blood from spattering the floor and walls.

Natasha examined her face in the mirror.

"What is this?" she asked.

"Eternal youth," Marianne said, her face looking like that of a teenager. "Imagine how old I must really be."

"Older than me," Natasha replied.

"Very much older. Older than you can ever imagine. One day you'll look back and you'll thank me."

Chapter Three

Change your environment; change your life.

Natasha Rearranges Her Environment

Natasha smiled at her face in the mirror. She thanked Marianne often. Every time she reread her diary entry about her encounter with Marianne, she was grateful to her Aunt Lydia and to Marianne.

Intuition.

She had to get going. Maggie and Ellie were going to kill her. She was always bugging them about being late and now here she was doing the same thing to them.

* * *

Maggie and Ellie were waiting for her at Intuition. The bar had recently been transformed into a jazz club with black tablecloths and candles. At the far end of the room, musicians played a slow, melodic tune. The platform elevated them so the patrons at tables farther back in the curve of the room could also see. Natasha recognized the old swing tune as it tingled through her bones.

"I'm so sorry," Natasha said as she pulled off her coat. She wore a long-sleeved, thigh-length, black turtleneck with a long, black leather skirt. A large white sapphire gleamed from a gold locket that hung on a heavy gold chain around her neck.

"No worries. I just got here myself," Maggie said as she scooted her chair a bit sideways to make room for Natasha. Maggie had long, wavy, red hair and friendly eyes. She was laughing, as they all knew how it was so unlike Natasha to be late for anything. "I was the first one here. Imagine that," Ellie said proudly. The women laughed louder, causing people at the nearby tables to turn their heads.

"Shhh, we're disturbing the music lovers," Maggie whispered as she giggled. She took a sip of beer and feigned interest in the band.

"Definitely something in the stars tonight," Natasha said. "So, how's the band?"

"Not bad," Ellie said. "The sax player is cute." The women turned their attention towards the curly-haired musician. He was a short, wiry man wearing dark sunglasses. In fact, the whole band wore sunglasses, adding to the funky jazz vibe their instruments were crooning.

"I think I like the drummer. Look how he holds those sticks," Maggie said, draining her glass. She reached for the pitcher and one of the clean glasses on the table. "Beer tonight, Natasha? "She asked as she tipped the pitcher to the mouth of the lass.

"Yes. Beer sounds good right about now." Natasha sipped the cold brew and turned to Ellie.

"Tell me, when will you come and *feng shui* my music room? Look what you did for Maggie."

31

Maggie was too engrossed in the music to listen to what the other women were talking about.

"So far, so good with her. I hope she can keep it up," Ellie said.

"Well, I'm not a clutter bug like her, that's for certain. I just want to know the best way to organize my instruments and music books."

"I'll have to look up a few things, like the most auspicious place for the recording equipment versus the instruments. Which one represents which element the most.

"I don't even want to know about elements and yin and yang and all that. I have too much in my head already." Natasha grinned.

"It's really fascinating when you look at it."

"I'm sure it is, honey. To you."

Ellie nodded and smiled. She was proud of her knowledge and knew Natasha was proud of her too. Ellie had come so far since they had first met.

In fact, Maggie had brought them together. They were two shy, withdrawn people who met the same chatty woman on the same night. Maggie met Ellie at the grocery store and Natasha at the bookstore and invited them for a girls' night out. They played pool and talked. After hanging out a few times, Natasha brought them to Lucy.

Lucy had been thrilled that her missing two members had been found. Only three months previously, two ladies had moved from Hermana, and her circle was no longer complete. The energy worked best when there were 12 ladies and herself. Once more, the universe had provided for the coven.

Ellie was so shy and withdrawn back then. She

barely looked at Lucy and seemed distant at the initiation ceremony. However, after a month had passed, her manner was noticeably different. Ellie had become bubbly and outgoing, although there were still times she retreated into hibernation. She discovered *feng shui* and after trying it out personally, she decided it was a viable path to follow. She drove to Boston for courses and, after gaining several certificates, launched her practice. She even *feng shui*ed the circle room at Lucy's home.

Now Natasha was hoping to use her services.

"I'll come over next week. Is that okay?" Ellie said.

"I'll check my book and we'll find a slot." Natasha nodded.

The music shifted into a louder and livelier beat. The women listened appreciatively, but Natasha soon grew weary of the jazz-fusion. She looked around the club and thought she saw a man watching her. His dark, beady eyes met hers, and he stared intently. Natasha was trying to figure out if she knew him when Maggie made a comment about the drummer. She looked at the stage to see who Maggie was talking about. When she looked back moments later, the dark-eyed man was gone. She shook her head and tried to enjoy the music.

When the musicians took a break, she turned to her friends.

"I'm sorry, ladies, but I've got to go."

"Oh, Natasha," Maggie whined. "We haven't even talked yet."

"I know. I'll see you soon."

Natasha kissed her friends on the cheek and

turned to leave. The guitar player stood in front of her. He had raised his sunglasses so his bright blue eyes were revealed. His tousled, blond hair was damp with sweat, and his face glowed.

"Hey, you're that woman who plays the violin," he said. "I'd recognize you anywhere."

"Yes, I play the violin."

"Do you want to come jam with us sometime? You're really good."

Natasha stared at him.

"Where did you see me?"

"All over the place. New Year's Eve in that quartet, of course. And at a couple of the clubs. You like to jam?"

"Sometimes. It depends on the band and if I know their repertoire."

"I bet you'd know some of ours."

"I don't really know jazz music," Natasha said.

The man laughed. "We play more than jazz. We can rock and roll too. Name's Craig."

"Well, nice to meet you, Craig. I'm Natasha."

"Seriously, we'd like to jam with you." Craig reached into his pocket and pulled out a business card. Natasha took it and put it in her purse.

"All right, Craig, I'll give you a call sometime."

Craig wandered off and found his friends. He winked at Natasha as she pushed the heavy doors open and retreated into the snow. She had enjoyed the warmth of the club, but it was too soon after all the New Year's festivities for her to party.

She walked along the dark, icy sidewalks, her thoughts drifting back to Gus. She had meant to ask her friends if they had ever seen him around before New Year's Eve, but the music had been too loud for conversation.

Maybe if Ellie *feng shui*ed her home, Gus would find her sooner.

* * *

"You have some really old pieces here. They must be worth a fortune," Ellie exclaimed as she looked at Natasha's shelves of instruments. Ellie and Natasha were standing in Natasha's loft. They had found openings in their schedules much earlier than Natasha had expected, and she was delighted they could get to work on activating better energy in her loft.

"Yes, some have been in the family for generations. I'm not sure if they have anything but sentimental value, but they are mine and I treasure them." Natasha had flipped on the bright overhead lights.

"Well, the first thing to go is that light," Ellie said. "Fluorescents and *feng shui* aren't the best mix. Especially when they're so damn bright."

"I rarely use them. I prefer practicing by candlelight." Natasha turned off overhead lights and activated the electric candles. "See? I only turned the brightest lights on so you could get a good look at the place."

"I see," Ellie said. "Yes, this electric candlelight is much better. But you're right, the room is too dim for us. Okay, put the fluorescents back on so we can see."

Natasha tapped the switches again.

"I like how you carpeted the walls and ceilings to soundproof it."

"It must work. I've never had people complain."

"Well, when it's warm and you have your window open, I can hear you on the street."

Natasha nodded. "I know. I play my best when I think people can hear me." She looked at Ellie expectantly. "So?"

"So, let's get to it." Ellie smiled.

Ellie spread out large pieces of paper with symbols and grids on them. She looked around the room and drew everything where she felt it would be most auspicious. She had a compass and protractor, colored pencils and a Chinese *feng shui* grid. Natasha paced, periodically peering over Ellie's shoulder as she drew and erased and drew again.

"Is it so important to draw it all first?" Natasha asked.

"Well, it's easier in this case as you have so many big items." When Ellie was done, she laid down her pencil. "Okay. Now comes the manual-labor part."

"I'm ready," Natasha said.

It took much effort to heave and pull the shelving, pianos and speakers around the room. After a lot of sweat and patient maneuvering, the women sat back and enjoyed the results of their labor.

"This looks much better," Natasha said.

"It feels much better, don't you think?" Ellie asked. She held up her hands. "You can practically feel the shift in the air currents."

"It's true."

Ellie pulled out a sage stick and a small, wrapped

bowl of sand from her bag. "Let's just sage the room and it should all be great."

The women walked around the room with the sage stick, chanting softly. They ran the smoke along the cases and shelves, being certain to cleanse the corners of the rooms even up to the ceilings. When they returned to the beginning of their circle, Ellie doused the stick in her bowl of sand.

"So, let the magic begin," she said.

After Ellie left, Natasha found her favorite violin and began to play. Her bow soared across the strings. Somehow the music seemed higher and sweeter than it ever had. The sound echoed through the room as if she were in the most magnificent concert hall.

She played until the sun came up, her thoughts straying now and again to Gus, and then back into the music again. Her nipples throbbed and her groin ached when she played. She imagined hands touching her, caressing her, pleasing her in unexpected ways. Her stomach growled with hunger. She was always hungry, it seemed, and she tried to ignore the sensation.

Her bow flew faster and, her fingers danced quickly as she funneled her longing and appetite into the instrument.

At last, she was exhausted, and after carefully wrapping her violin back up in its padded blanket and putting it back into its case, she went to bed.

Chapter Four

Beware of strangers. They may not be who they seem.

Séance

Natasha pulled up to the front of the old house at 11:30. It had been a short drive from Hermana, which she didn't mind as she sang along to the radio. The air was thick with love songs, trying to get everyone in the mood for Valentine's Day even though the New Year had barely begun.

This woman was old money, and the house had been in the family for generations. Babies had been born here, and a few old folks had died in their beds over the decades. As Natasha stood out front staring at the huge turrets, she imagined all the love found and lost between those walls. The sensation of a mostly happy home reached out to her from the painted wooden slats. Her feet danced up the stairs, and she approached the front door with giddiness.

Darkness suddenly rushed through her. Turning her head, she tried to see the shadow that flitted from the corner of her eye. However, there was nothing there. The dizziness passed and she caught her breath.

She shrugged and rang the bell.

Clara Farnsworth opened the door. She was a tall, well-coiffed woman with bright red hair and large rhinestone earrings. Her mauve pantsuit glowed in the porch light.

"Natasha. Right on time," she said as she took Natasha's coat. "I set the table up in here." She took Natasha to a dining room where there was a large oak table. Several chairs were placed around it. There were two large white pillar candles on either side.

"Perfect," Natasha said.

"Fabulous. Come in. I'll have you meet my guests."

Natasha shook hands with Mr. and Mrs. Hill, Jeannette Summers, Keith Gladstone and Ian Ferguson. When she touched the hand of Jim Hawthorne, she flinched instinctively.

"Sorry. Carpet shock," she said as she rubbed her hand in mock pain.

"Never mind," Clara said. "We've work to do. Let's get ready; it's almost time."

By midnight, everyone was settled in and lightly touching hands. Jim Hawthorne sat across from Natasha, and she kept looking over at him as she led the group in meditation. The surge of the energy in the circle vibration began to buzz beneath her fingers. She could feel all the circuits connecting between each set of hands until they stopped cold at Jim.

"Everyone, please close your eyes. Really try to focus," Natasha said, somewhat harshly. She silently commanded the circle to continue around, but it couldn't pass through him. She willed the energy to jump past him, yet it wouldn't. She sighed. There was always one at every séance. Natasha teased the energy as high as she could get it to go. When at last the vibration seemed high enough, she was ready.

"Who do you want to call, Clara?" Natasha asked.

"Percy Lipchuck. He was my great uncle. He died in the bed upstairs in the second guestroom."

Natasha nodded and called Percy.

"Knock three times if you're here," she urged. The candles flickered. The circle sat expectantly. In the dim candlelit room, Clara's eyes shimmered brightly with fear and expectation.

Mr. and Mrs. Hill looked at each other. Jim Hawthorne sat with his eyes squeezed shut. Three very soft knocks were heard.

Jeannette gasped while Keith nearly pulled his hand away in fear.

"I hope there's no one else in the house. There shouldn't be," Clara said, looking around.

"I don't know if that's good or bad," Keith sighed.

"Shh," Jeannette said. "You wanted to come to this."

There was a shift in the energy around Natasha. Darkness hovered over her shoulder. Mrs. Hill looked at her, eyes glistening in the candlelight.

"There's something around you, Natasha," she said softly.

"I feel it too," Natasha said. "There are a few people here tonight."

"Is Uncle Percy here?" Clara asked.

Natasha closed her eyes and tried to hear through the babbling voices that suddenly took up residence in her head. They weren't speaking words, per se; it was more like feelings. She reached further in to find Uncle Percy. At last, he ebbed forth. His spirit was weak but present nonetheless.

"He's here," Natasha announced.

Clara sighed with relief. "Finally. You don't know how many…"

"Shhhh…" Jeannette said, tossing her perfectly coiffed dark hair. "Ask him something."

Clara gave Jeannette a nasty look and turned her attention to Natasha. "Ask him if he was poisoned."

It was Jeannette's turn to start talking. "Clara…you never…."

"Shh," Mrs. Hill said.

"Percy, were you murdered?" Natasha asked. She tried to find Percy again, but the blackness interfered.

"What is it?" Mr. Hill asked.

"Nothing. Give me a second." Natasha closed her eyes and tried to focus, yet every time, the wall of darkness blocked her.

"Everyone," Natasha said, "everyone in this room, in this circle, must open up to the greatness of our universe. If you don't open yourself up, no one can come through the portal." She breathed deeply. "Everyone. Breathe with me. In time to my counting. Keep your feet planted flat on the floor. We're trying to create a complete circuit, a portal for the other side to come through." Her words were slow and low. She breathed rhythmically, and everyone followed suit.

The energy in the room grew softer, and Uncle Percy ebbed into her mind again.

"Percy, were you murdered?" Natasha asked. The missing link in the circle made Percy's connection unclear. She would have had better luck by herself, but

41

they were paying her to experience a ghost for themselves.

Natasha felt her hair being lifted and dropped, fondled, and tangled between unseen fingers. Her shoulders were heavy, as if there were a weight pressed down upon them. Her head dropped forward, and energy surged through her hands.

"Oh," Mrs. Hill said to her left. "Your hands are so hot."

Natasha could hear her but she couldn't respond. She was in the grip of some force, and she let it take her over.

"Yes," Natasha said in a voice that wasn't hers. "I was murdered."

Natasha bolted upright and blinked. She stared around the room, her head foggy and her body buzzing.

"What happened? "she asked.

"You brought someone in, but we don't know who," said Clara.

"It wasn't Percy?"

"I don't think so. It was not him," said Ian.

Natasha sighed. "I think that's enough for tonight. We shall close the circle now."

"Do we have to?" Clara asked.

"I don't have the strength to continue," Natasha said.

Jeannette looked over at the large clock on the wall." She has been doing this for over an hour."

"Gosh, has it been that long? It didn't seem that long," Keith said.

As Natasha regained her strength, she looked over at Jim Hawthorne. He was staring at her, and she wasn't sure what he was trying to see.

"Let's close the portal," Natasha said. They all held hands as she thanked the spirits and asked them to leave Clara in peace. She was dizzy and weak but knew it would pass.

Once Natasha was out in the chilly night air, she felt better. Still, the hunger surged through her. It was time to feed again. Properly. But not just yet. She was a master at putting off her desires, including her sexual ones. She figured she should get a prize for self-denial when she died. If she ever died.

She drove slowly through the icy roads until at last she arrived back at her loft. She was drained, but she didn't feel like going home yet. She parked the car in her parking spot and donned her hat and gloves.

It was very late, but as she walked through the downtown strip of Hermana, she saw many of the pubs were still crowded. It never seemed to matter which day of the week it was; the little town was full of people who liked to socialize.

She passed by Intuition and heard lively jazz music playing as someone opened the door to leave the club. She decided to go in for a nightcap.

If there had been a crowd that night, it had thinned. She took a seat near the stage and saw Craig had seen her come in. He grinned as he met her eyes, and she knew she had done the right thing by coming there.

The waitress brought her a glass of wine, and she sipped it, trying to let the vibes of the séance recede back to wherever they needed to go. The music soothed her, which was surprising since she wasn't a very big fan of jazz.

When the last song was finished, the audience clapped politely. The band packed up their instruments

43

for the night. As the drummer and sax player wound up the cables and put away the mics, Craig came over to her table.

"Mind if I have a seat?" he asked.

"Not at all," she said. "I was hoping you'd ask."

He sat down and, before long, the waitress brought them both a drink. Craig nodded at the waitress.

"Thanks." He turned to Natasha. "I took the liberty of ordering another round for us."

"Why are you out so late? And alone?" he asked.

"I had a job tonight. A séance out of town. Thought I'd drop in for a nightcap."

"I'm very glad you did. I've been thinking about you."

"And I've been thinking about you too," Natasha said. "About what you said."

"Jamming? You interested?" Craig asked.

"Yes, I am," Natasha said. "In fact, I have an urge to play tonight."

"Well, I'm up for it. If you want to do guitar and violin. I'm not sure the other guys are in at this late hour, since they have girlfriends to get home to and all."

"That's fine. I've done it before. Just with guitar, I mean." She grinned.

"Where do you want to go? Do you want to go to my place?" Craig asked.

"We might as well go to mine. I have a studio, and my violin is there," Natasha said.

"Very well."

They finished their drinks, and Craig grabbed his guitar case. They walked through the icy, cold streets until they were back at Natasha's home. She decided she'd take him up the back stairwell through the door that led directly to the music room.

"Very nice," Craig said as she flipped on the electric candles. "This is an amazing studio."

"You like it?" she asked. "I'm quite proud of it."

Craig went over to the shelf and looked at her many instruments. "What kind of guitar is that?" he asked, pointing to a closed case.

"Open it up and try it out," Natasha urged. "I'll get us some wine."

Craig's face was flushed with excitement as he opened up the guitar case. Natasha left the room and went into her living area as he oohed and ahhed with delight as he tuned the guitar.

She gathered some wine, glasses and several types of cheese and crackers. When she returned to the room, Craig had the guitar plugged into an amp and was strumming it.

"What a lovely sound," he said. "This guitar is nicer than all of mine put together."

"I do take pride in my instruments," Natasha said.

"I'm glad. Because people like me certainly appreciate it."

She poured the wine, and Craig set down the guitar to take a glass.

"Let's toast to new jamming partners," he said.

"Let's." Natasha grinned as they clicked their glasses together. As they sipped their wine, she studied Craig. He was a pleasant enough fellow, his blue eyes bright, his blond hair curly, but he had a rather weak chin. He was slender, slight and his knee bounced with nervous energy. He wasn't as handsome as Gus, but

45

Gus wasn't here. Gus was far more masculine, with a strong jaw and eyes that held many secrets. Craig's eyes were curious and lively.

"Flattery will get you everywhere," Natasha said. "Okay, how do you want to do "Are you a Gemini?" she asked.

"Why, yes, I am. Hey, how did you know?"

"Just part of what I do," Natasha said as she sipped her wine.

"What about you?"

"Capricorn."

"Oh. That's right now, isn't it? Did you just have a birthday?"

"Not yet. Very soon," she said.

"Nice. Another year older," he said. "Here's to your impending birthday." He clinked his glass against hers again.

"Let's not rush it. I'm not so eager to get any older."

"Well, it's not going to catch up to you for a while. You can't be 30 yet," he said.

"I can read music or we can just jam," Craig said eagerly. "I know these days it's hard to find guitar players that can actually read."

"Yes, it does seem to be a dying art," she said. "However, you came here to jam, so let's jam."

Natasha busied herself with preparing her violin while Craig returned to the guitar. "Can I play yours?" he asked.

"Of course. Whatever you want."

It didn't take long before they were playing with and around each other. The music soared through a wide variety of styles as they egged each other on. One minute they were playing folk, the next they were rocking. Their fingers flew as the sounds from the strings filled the air.

At last, Natasha put down her violin. "That was great," she said.

"Yes, it was," Craig responded, his eyes shining with the exuberance of a session that had gone well.

"We should do it again sometime," she said.

"Yes, we should."

They stared awkwardly at each other until Craig leaned over to kiss her. At first, Natasha was reluctant, but as his lips pursued hers, she fell into him.

They kissed passionately in the music room, the vibrations of their jamming still hanging in the air. She could feel the music still swelling through Craig; he loved music as much as she did. She held him tightly, the gnawing in her stomach rumbling loudly.

Craig pulled back.

"Are you hungry?" he asked.

"Just for you," she said.

"Are you sure? Why don't you take a moment to eat?" he asked, reaching for the cheese tray.

"No, that won't help my hunger. Kiss me again. Your lips feel so good on mine."

Craig pulled her close again and let his mouth merge with hers. His tongue wiggled into her mouth, and she played with it gently. Craig's hands roamed up her back and down again to clutch her round bottom.

He was growing hard—she could feel him pressing against her. She rubbed into him, and they swayed, kissing and holding each other as if dancing to an invisible band.

"Over here," Natasha said and led him to a large velvet couch. She sat on it and pulled him down on top of her. He kissed her some more, his slight, thin body wriggling over her. She touched his back, his small bottom, and sighed. His smell was in her nostrils, and her stomach cried out again.

"Ignore it," she said as he lifted up from her. She took the moment to unbutton his shirt and toss it on the floor. He had many tattoos of vines, skulls and mythical creatures along his chest and arms. "Oh, let me see," she said, pushing him up.

He grinned. "You like tattoos?"

"I admire the artwork. I don't have one, but I think it's cool when other people do."

He stood up and modeled for her, turning around so she could see the wings and fire on his back.

"You're an angel?" she asked.

"Or a demon. Whichever you prefer," he joked.

"Mmm, what else do you have?"

Craig took her encouragement as an opportunity to slide off his jeans. He stood naked before her, his penis standing nearly fully erect.

"So, what do you have to show me?" he asked after she studied him for a while.

She grinned and sat up. "I can show you what I have to offer." Natasha said, removing her own clothes. She stood up naked in front of him. He admired her full breasts and touched her hard nipples. He ran his hand down her flat stomach to her shaved pubic area. His fingers touched her pussy lips and parted them. Natasha sighed, hunger of all kinds consuming her.

"Mmm," she said as his fingers found her clit. He pressed on it rhythmically, and she was reminded of the way they'd danced along the fingerboards. His expertise on her body was just as pleasing.

They kissed again, and her hand found his cock. She stroked him firmly, feeling him swell even more between her fingers.

"So lovely," he sighed. "So beautiful and so skilled."

Natasha kneeled down and took his cock into her mouth. She slowly teased his head with her tongue, swirling it around as he danced from one foot to the other.

"Suck me," he whispered.

She took him all the way into her mouth and sucked him hard, pulling him in and out with her hand. His legs shook as she teased him by varying her rhythms.

"Oh my God, you're so delicious," he said. "I want to fuck you right now."

He reached for his jeans to get out his condoms. She let him, even though she knew it wasn't necessary.

She lay back on the couch, her legs spread. He took in the vision before he climbed on top of her. His mouth met hers as he slid his cock into her damp, waiting pussy.

It had been a long time since she'd been fucked, and she savored the sensation of him filling her up. She wrapped her arms around him, wishing the little, wiry man was her big, strong Gus. But Gus wasn't here. She didn't even know if she would ever see Gus again. Although, on some dark level, she knew that the games between them weren't over yet.

Craig pushed into her slowly and moaned as he slid in and out. Natasha spread her legs wider, trying to pull him in farther. She wrapped her hands around his ass, pushing him in to the hilt.

"Oh, you like it deep, don't you?" he asked.

"Fill me up, Craig," she whispered.

Craig pushed her legs up so he could enter her more deeply. His lips met hers, and he pushed harder and faster. Craig had her pinned under him, and she let him take the lead as he pumped. His rhythmic movements built up to an energetic, frenzied fucking.

"More," she called out. "Faster, harder."

He laid into her harder, his neck by her mouth. She smelled him, the sweaty man smell that tingled her nose and made her hungrier. It would be so easy to just turn her head slightly and sink her teeth into him.

But she couldn't.

She had to resist. Her head spun. "Fuck me, Craig. Fuck me hard."

He slammed into her, fast and furious. They both moaned and cried as they reveled in the tension and suspension of holding back their climaxes. At last, Natasha could stand it no more and let herself release.

"Oh my God," she cried out. "I'm coming."

"Come on me, Natasha. Come on me," he cried as his own climax washed over him. He collapsed on her for a moment as he emptied himself into the condom, into her. She felt his twitches and smiled.

At last he eased himself out of her. He leaned over to kiss her. "You are magnificent," he said. "A great violinist and a great lover."

"You were fabulous too," Natasha said.

Her stomach growled loudly.

"You need to eat," he said. "Eat something."

"I will. I will. Later. I want to savor the moment."

They sat on the couch for a few moments, holding each other and sipping another glass of wine.

The silence was welcome as exhaustion held them both in its grip.

"I guess I should get going," Craig said. "It's probably almost morning by now."

"Yes, I need to get some sleep." Natasha yawned.

Craig put his clothes back on. He got his guitar and turned to face her. "We should do this again."

"Which? The jamming or the sex?" she playfully asked.

"Both." He laughed.

"Maybe we will."

Once he was gone, Natasha sat in her music room for a few more minutes. At least she had been able to quiet one of her hungers for the moment. But the other hunger made her restless, and she knew she wouldn't be able to sleep very well.

Reluctantly, she headed for the bedroom. The ghosts were waiting, as always, and through her annoyance, she was able to block them out.

For a little while, at least.

Chapter Five

A partnership may lead to new beginnings.

Kelly Proctor

Before Natasha left the house, she reviewed her diary and checked her horoscope. The diary helped her to remember events, and her horoscope spoke of partnerships. Kelly Proctor had lived a long and torturous life under the iron fists of her father and stepmother. In the early 1900's, Hermana had less than 500 residents, plus a seasonal influx of another 500 or so tourists and shippers. The town was growing, and in the summertime, the sound of hammers and saws were heard over the roar of the ocean. Houses were built, babies were born, people moved away and new people replaced them.

The deliveries made by water were often shady shipments of contraband smuggled in from larger docks by varying degrees of riffraff. The person in charge of the docks and, therefore, in control of the ring was Kelly's father, Edwin Proctor.

Kelly's birth had been the result of carelessness during a drunken date with a visiting girl named

Trinity. Once Trinity had realized she was carrying the evil older man's baby, she was beside herself. She went to him for help, and he took her in, much to everyone's surprise. When the baby came, he was the proudest father that ever was. Trinity went on to bear him two more children before her untimely death.

No one ever found out how she died in her bed one morning. She had been fine one day. And the next, she was gone.

Edwin didn't take long to replace Trinity with Marguerite, a fiery Spanish woman who had different ways than his. She was cold to the children, yet she and Edwin were together until husband and wife were found dead on a hot September day. Their heads had been smashed in with some sort of instrument. There were no suspects, but Kelly had behaved oddly that day.

The summer had already been unbearable. The headlines were rampant with musings about the murders of Mr. and Mrs. Borden over in Fall River. Had it been churchgoing, hard-working daughter Lizzie who had killed them? The speculations were the entertainment of the summer.

When the double-murder tragedy struck in Hermana, in a house that had already stored a wealth of horrors, people wondered if Kelly, too, had been pushed to the edge.

Natasha learned that Kelly's life may have looked glamorous to the outside world, yet in reality, her dear old dad was a big old thug, and his actions were monstrous. Daily routines were set to a tee. There was no room for error or lateness. Breakfast was served like clockwork. There were errands for Kelly and household chores, such as laundry and shopping.

Kelly had learned at a young age that her father was a crook, and the only reason she kept living with him until she was in her thirties was because she was afraid of what might happen if she ever left his protection. His protection had a price, though. Lateness and sloppiness resulted in spankings. Other forms of misconduct, real or imagined, caused him to lock her in a closet, or worse, in the basement.

Marguerite was always finding new ways to punish Kelly, and Edwin never questioned her.

There were more little zigzags in the story. Natasha knew she would learn plenty on the guided house tour. She remembered Kelly and her parents from her diaries. She definitely remembered Edwin.

In his prime, Edwin had been a dashing, handsome man. The reason he got away with his outrageous behavior lay more in his bewitching Scorpio eyes than in any fear he instilled.

Natasha had been walking along the docks, long ago, watching the birds, when she saw him walking toward her the other way.

"What are you doing here?" he asked her harshly. "I'm just going for walk," Natasha said.

"Can't. Private property." He pointed to the No Trespassing sign. "Oh. Since when? I come by here a lot."

"For about a month. I bought it." He stood proudly, his face still dark and menacing. At the time, she judged him to be in his early fifties. His salt-and-pepper hair fell in curls to his shoulders; his forehead had the deep wrinkles of a man who touched the sea on a daily basis.

"Sorry." She turned to go back the way she'd come, and he caught her arm.

"Wait." He held her as he looked deeply into her eyes. His rough forwardness gave her a thrill. Her teeth itched at the thought of one so feisty.

"Why don't you continue on?" He looked out toward the ocean and squinted. The horizon was empty except for swirling seagulls playing around lobster buoys. He looked back at her. "I'll walk with you."

His talk was sweet, his seductions simple, and it wasn't long before a drink of whiskey in his hut led to a tumble in the tiny bedroom. He was forceful, and she let him have his way at first. As her hunger grew, she couldn't help but push him back and firmly latch herself to him

with her pussy, all the while staring into his eyes. His hardness swelled in her, and she raised and lowered her hips, drawing him in deeper. She leaned over, nuzzling at his neck, biting and sucking on the salty fluid that pulsed into her mouth.

"You're rough," he muttered, losing himself in his thrusts. She drank a bit more, pressed her fingers over the wound and let her pussy take over the rest of her feast.

She came with a groan, sensation fanning through her so intensely that she threw her head back. The sight of his blood dripping from her mouth and her chin upset him so greatly that he pushed her off.

He jumped off the bed, grabbing the blanket to cover himself up. He was shaking as he screamed.

"What the hell are you?" he asked. "What have you done?"

"I'm sorry," she said, batting her eyelashes at him. "I got a little rough." She wiped her mouth with the back of her hand.

"You must have a helluva set of teeth to draw blood like that. Why don't you go clean yourself up now?"

"I'll give you a blowjob when I get back," she said playfully. "Uh, no, thanks," he said. "I think I've had enough."

While she was washing up, he muttered while he examined his wound in the hall mirror. She smiled as she enjoyed the feeling of fullness, at least for a moment.

Edwin Proctor's smuggling business turned a great profit, and it wasn't long before he made enough to buy a house and run a legal business importing goods from China and the Middle East.

Natasha fed from him twice more over the years. As he grew older, she never aged. Her beauty always shocked him. He was a man who liked to act on impulse, and he didn't worry about little things like being married.

It would be strange to go to the house where he was murdered. A murder unsolved to that very day.

Madeline had been aching to stay over in the house, the whole house, to see what she could pick up. She was a real ghost hunter, while Natasha was a medium. Madeline had always felt that they could work well together. This evening would be the first time they joined forces.

Natasha and Madeline knew each other from Lucy's circle. Madeline was a bubbly Aquarian, rather skittish, and Natasha often wondered why she'd chosen ghost-hunting as her profession.

Madeline had rented one of the rooms for the night. The owner reluctantly ran a bed and breakfast that was mostly frequented by repeat clients. Ghost stories abounded about the house, although many other houses in Hermana were similarly haunted. Natasha thought about her own loft and the growing number of spirits who seemed to be taking up residence in it.

As Natasha walked up the creaky porch stairs, she though back to how the house had first looked when it was built. Shiny and new. Trinity and then Marguerite could often be seen with the children out in the front or coming and going from their many errands. The children grew up, and two left home while the strange and likely crazy Kelly remained a spinster until she died in that house.

A chill ran through Natasha as she thought about Kelly. She paused on the porch steps and looked out at the street. The main downtown area of Hermana was two blocks over. The snow was falling steadily, and the glow of the lamplight created shadows from the tall, twisted trees that framed the driveway. As she stared at them, remembering when they were only tiny twigs in the ground, a shadow moved beyond the hedge. She squinted, trying to identify it. Her head began to throb, and she knew that it was no animal. The shadow fled to the side of the hedges and set off down the street, hugging the foliage until he was far from sight.

The feeling of unease continued as her thoughts about dead Kelly returned.

There were many times that stories about Kelly swept through the town. After her parents died, she continued to live in the house. Many speculated about the reasons. Perhaps she had indeed killed them and now gloated at the thought of them every day. Perhaps she was too attached to the house to leave it. She had never been one for adventure and travel.

As Natasha thought about it over the decades, she surmised that Kelly didn't move because victims of abuse are often attached to things that cause them pain.

Kelly became rather wild after her parents died. She was known to hold parties that lasted for days. Fancy cars came and went. Music and noise emitted from the house that had stood quiet since it had been built.

Kelly died when she was old, with a pile of cats. She partied right up until that day. Her companion, Lady Marisha, who had been traveling with a circus until she discovered love in Hermana, was the one who found her.

Funny, Natasha thought. *Here they are calling her a spinster when the old lady probably had more action than anyone. People just ignored the existence of Lady Marisha. Lesbians didn't exist back in the day.*

Madeline had already arrived. When the front door opened, she bolted in from the living room, clutching her camera.

"It's so weird to be here with no one else," Madeline said. "So creepy."

"It is." Natasha stared wide-eyed around the house, the furnishings still intact from the day it made history for the supposed copycat double murder.

The air shifted around her, as if urging her inside with curling tendrils of hot and cold. The busy pattern of the carpet combined with the patterns of the raised, velvet wallpaper made her head spin.

"You're back." The voice was loud in her head. Male. Stern.

Edwin's.

"Oh…" Natasha sat down in the closest chair as her knees grew weak. Whisperings and whining whistled through her head as if a classroom of children were arguing. The whisperings of the house invaded all her thoughts, and she looked up at Madeline with wide eyes.

"What is it?" Madeline asked.

"There's a lot of them here." Natasha nodded. "Ask them something."

"Like what?"

"Maybe who did the murder?"

"I'm sure they get asked that all the time."

Madeline looked around the room, shooting off her camera. "Do you think they would answer?"

Natasha closed her eyes. "Who murdered you, Edwin?"

The room grew hot. Madeline stared at Natasha holding herself. The camera hung loosely in her fingers.

"What's happening? The air is so thick and so hot," Madeline said.

"I know." Natasha's cheeks were burning as the air continued to swell with heat and humidity.

"I'm drenched," Madeline said. "Hell, it's January. This place was freezing when we got here."

"It's why there's no point in getting air conditioning," a voice said from the hallway. Natasha and Madeline jumped as they looked over at Mrs. Cookson, the current owner of the property. "You'll see. One minute you're looking for your coat, the next you want to run around naked."

"You scared the hell out of me," Madeline said. "God, you're quiet."

"Sorry. I tend to scare guests a lot. In a way, it's kind of fun," she said as she patted the bun in her hair. Mrs. Cookson was dressed in a period outfit from the twenties. The simple gray dress with a white cotton apron and her severe hairstyle. seemed a contrast to her cheerful demeanor. Natasha presumed she was in her late fifties, but she couldn't tell.

Mrs. Cookson had secrets. Natasha could sense it. Most people did. Natasha wondered what Mrs. Cookson had seen in the house that she wasn't sharing.

"Have you seen anything here?" Natasha asked.

"Oh, certainly. In fact, I'll tell you all about it on our tour. Would you like some coffee before we start?"

"Tea?" Natasha asked.

"Coffee for me," Madeline said.

Mrs. Cookson led them into the kitchen, which was a simple affair with a huge wood-burning oven and a microwave on the counter. The coffee and tea had already been poured into thermal canisters, and Mrs. Cookson led them into a dining room. She placed the tray on a long table covered with a flowered tablecloth with a white doily on top.

Natasha picked up swells of different personalities throughout the rooms. Sadness was the dominant feeling, but there was a lot of anger as well.

Most of the anger was masculine.

Most of it seemingly from Edwin himself.

What do you want?" Natasha asked him in her mind. There was only heat again, and she willed him away in her mind so she could enjoy her tea. A cup rolled across the table and fell onto the floor.

"That would be the children," Mrs. Cookson said as she settled into a chair.

"Sit."

Madeline took one of the cookies Mrs. Cookson offered and prepared her coffee. "Children?"

"No one's proven there are really children. Sometimes I think it's the Proctor children enjoying a happy childhood instead of the grim lives they ended up living once Edwin married Marguerite."

"What was her deal? Why was she so evil?" Madeline asked.

"Was she evil?" Mrs. Cookson asked. "Or was it the way of her country? To punish so severely."

"I'm not convinced it's really the way of any country. To lock up grown people because they drop a dish or look at a boy in church? There's more to it," Madeline said.

The air grew more menacing, and the undercurrent of rage surged through Natasha's being. "Uh," Natasha said as she stood up. "Let's change the subject. The spirits aren't amused."

"You do have to be careful what you say in the house. Sometimes accidents happen."

With that, Mrs. Cookson mimed zipping up her lips and waved for them to follow her lead into the front room.

Natasha and Madeline finished their coffee, leaving their cups on the table.

Mrs. Cookson began the tour, leading the ladies through the 11 rooms in the two-story house. She explained where walls had been installed or moved to allow the house to be more functional as a bed and breakfast.

"It's an odd business, this bed and breakfast stuff. You don't want too many weirdos coming through, yet at the same time, you don't want to sit around with an empty house and no one to pay the bills. You can tell by how the air changes so quickly that the furnace goes nuts trying to keep up."

"Is this Kelly?" Natasha asked, picking up a picture. A woman with sullen eyes stared back at her. The hurt and despair in those eyes pricked her through the heart. She remembered passing those eyes on the streets so many decades ago. The same eyes as her father, except his held hate and disdain. "She was beaten a lot," Natasha said as she put down the picture.

"Some suggest she was disciplined harshly," Mrs. Cookson said, pointing into the air.

Natasha nodded, understanding her gesture.

"Right. Funny how sad she looks and yet she's in the middle of a party," Madeline observed.

Natasha looked again and noticed with a jolt that there were other people in the picture as well. A pretty blonde clutched Kelly's arm, and she looked to be about 20 years younger than the mature Kelly. There were several handsome, strong-jawed men and a person whose gender was difficult to determine. Natasha figured it must be a transvestite. The picture had been taken in the living room downstairs. The same living room where the father had been murdered. The stepmother had been taken out in the kitchen.

"There's a lot of grief in this house. Well, more than three people."

"Four," Madeline reminded her. "The first wife, the second wife, Edwin and Kelly. "And that's what people know about," Mrs. Cookson said. "Some say things went on in the basement. People who crossed Edwin or owed him money. There was even talk of some kind of torture equipment down there."

62

"Probably Marguerite tying Edwin to a spank table and letting him have it," Natasha joked. Mrs. Cookson looked crossly at her.

"Don't you dare," she warned. "Don't mock him. "It's okay," Natasha said. "I can handle him."

"Don't say I didn't warn you."

Shortly after that, Mrs. Cookson came to the end of her stories and was yawning. "It's so late, ladies. I really need to get to bed."

"You can sleep in this place?" Madeline asked, rubbing her arms, which were peppered with goose bumps.

"Of course. I live here, don't I?" Mrs. Cookson smiled, and for a moment, Natasha wasn't sure if the woman wasn't a reincarnation of Kelly herself.

"Were you ever connected to any of them?" Natasha asked.

"Oh Lord, no. And thank goodness," she whispered. The lights in the room flickered.

Madeline and Natasha carried their suitcases to their respective rooms. Madeline chose Kelly's room, and Natasha took Edwin's.

"You and I, back together again," she joked.

The sudden heat in the air wasn't lost on her, but she wasn't frightened. He could bluster at her as much as he wanted, but she wouldn't get hurt.

How could she get hurt? She had eternal life.

She put on a long, white nightgown and went to find Madeline. First, she checked Kelly's room, but Madeline wasn't there.

After walking through the house, she found Madeline back downstairs in the living room, clicking her camera in the corners of the ceiling.

"What are you doing? Looking for orbs?" Natasha asked. Her sudden presence startled Madeline.

"Yes. God, you sneak around worse than the ghosts!"

"I didn't sneak, but I guess I should have made more noise so as not to startle you," Natasha said.

"You know, there might be things here that could really be captured by proper equipment. I'm going to try to get a team in here sometime."

"That would be interesting. But don't you think the more people you bring in, the more the ghosts will hide?"

"You're the medium. What do you think?" Natasha sat down on the couch. "Oh, it could go either way."

"That's how it always is." Madeline sat down next to her. "So what do you think? Should we try to do a séance?"

"We can if you want, but there are no answers here tonight," Natasha said. Madeline frowned in disappointment. "What do you mean there are no answers here?"

"I can tell the ghosts don't want to talk today."

"How? You haven't even tried."

Natasha leaned toward Madeline. "In my experience, if the ghosts want to talk, they make themselves known to me. I don't have to go through all the shenanigans of a séance and calling them. They just come. Anywhere. Anytime."

"Really?"

"Oh, yes."

"You're not just saying that because you're tired?"

"No, not at all. There are things here, yes. Angry spirits and resonance, but they aren't going to talk tonight."

"So this is all pointless?"

"Yes. Today it is. Maybe we should get Gwen to draw up some astrological charts to help us determine the best time to call them. Some aspects are more auspicious than others. Maybe the birth charts of the victims in relevance to planetary alignments?"

"Do you really think so?"

"Today I think so. Yes." Natasha stared around the room. There were spirits here, but they weren't going to tell Madeline what she needed to hear. Natasha didn't feel like getting into all the details of her reasoning. The pull of Edwin was strong, and she wasn't sure Madeline could cope if Natasha were to bring him in at a séance. Not while he was still raging against Natasha.

"Have you gotten any orbs today?" Natasha asked.

Madeline pressed the Review button on her camera and stared into the viewfinder. "Hmmm. yes, there are a few. There are some strange mists and things. The usual stuff I get in this house."

"Why don't you just try to get some sleep? See if anything comes to you in the night.""I don't know if I want anything to come to me in the night. I'm kind of nervous."

"Then when you go to bed, tell them you don't want them bugging you."

"I'll try that."

"Good." Natasha hugged her. "I'm sorry to be such a drag. But that's how it is. We can't always be in sync with the spirits."

"I know. If anyone knows that, it's me."

"Then, goodnight." Natasha stood. "I'm going to go to bed."

Natasha made her way back up the stairs. The hairs on the back of her neck stood on end as she felt Edwin's presence follow her back to his room. She knew she had to answer to him before anything else could be done in the house.

The room was stifling hot as she lay down in the double bed. She turned off the lamp and lay in the darkness. She wondered how a big man like Edwin Proctor could share such a bed with Marguerite, but she imagined he didn't share it often with her, knowing his habits as she did.

It didn't take long for him to appear. His eyes were more piercing than they had been in life as he approached her bed.

"Natasha," he said, his voice a gravelly, disembodied sound. "You've come back to me."

"No, I haven't, Edwin. I'm only here to help my friend."

"You don't help anyone but yourself. You know that," he said.

"It takes one to know one," Natasha whispered.

Edwin floated over to her until he was beside the bed. He touched her cheek. "Pretty Natasha. You still haven't aged. Tell me your secret."

"Good living. Something you know nothing about. Or knew nothing about, I should say," she retorted, brushing his hand away.

"Come now, Natasha. Don't be like that. We had some good times."

"Yes, we did. When you were alive."

"And we can again."

His essence grew more solid, and the air shifted from stifling hot to freezing cold. Natasha tried to burrow under the covers, but he tore them off.

"Now, now, Natasha. No need to hide from me," Edwin cooed. "It can be like old times."

"No, it can't," she said. "Unless…"

"Yes?"

"If I let you have your way with me, will you be certain to give Madeline her information when she comes back next time?"

Edwin laughed. The sound was ghastly and hurt Natasha's ears. "You always have a price, don't you? That's my Natasha."

"Everyone has a price. I don't think it's too much to ask, do you?" Natasha said as she sat up against the pillows. She untied the bow that closed her nightgown and spread the material open so he could see her breasts.

"I think we can arrange something," he said as he lowered his face to kiss her cleavage. The room shifted to hot again as his burning lips touched her flesh. The sensation was

blissfully pleasant, and she opened her gown further. He nuzzled down into her. "Oh, Natasha, how I've missed you," he sighed.

"I doubt that," she said.

"I don't miss how you liked to bite me. And you can't now," he sneered. "I know. See what I'm giving up for you?"

He reached for her breasts and stroked them, teasing at her nipples until they were hard. She lay back on the pillows as he fondled her.

"Have you ever fucked a ghost before?" he asked.

"Ladies don't kiss and tell," she replied.

"Very well." His voice was angry, as if he had been betrayed. "Please, you think you're the only ghost I see or feel?"

"I'm not?"

"I'm a medium, Edwin. I can see and feel things that would make most people freak out and die."

"You talk too much, Natasha," he said as he clasped a hand over her mouth. He tweaked one of her nipples roughly. "You also have too many clothes on."

Natasha sat up and shimmied the nightgown off over her head. She tossed it to the floor. "There, is that better?" she asked, lying back and spreading her legs so he could see her pussy.

"Much better," he said as he bent over to taste her. The sensation of his tongue on her clit was very real, yet strangely electric. His anger made him rough, but she still enjoyed him. She raised her hips to meet him.

"You like it. You're quivering," he said with satisfaction, looking up at her.

"You always were good at eating me," she said, forcing his face back down to continue what he'd started.

"You were always the tastiest. So many women never bothered to wash properly back then. It was most..."

"Enough," Natasha said. "Get busy."

Edwin continued to lick her, his ethereal tongue and fingers working magic in a way his living being hadn't been capable of. Before long, Natasha was shuddering with a climax. Her legs twitched, and Edwin stood back.

"That was just the beginning," he said as he lay on top of her. His spirit cock was huge and penetrated her with an icy coldness. She cried out in glorious pleasure-pain.

"Oh!"

There was a knock at her door.

"Natasha?" Madeline's voice called out. "Are you okay?"

"Just a minute." Natasha snapped on the lamp.

Edwin vanished. Natasha went over to the door to let Madeline in, scooping up her nightgown to cover herself as she pulled open the door.

"I heard you call out," Madeline said sheepishly. "I didn't know if you'd seen a ghost."

"Oh, I must have been dreaming," Natasha said. "Don't worry. I talk in my sleep."

Madeline came in and sat on her bed. The room grew very hot as Edwin's frustration engulfed it.

"Boy, it's hot in here. How can you sleep at all?"

"I'm tired. You know. When you're tired, you can sleep through anything."

"Maybe you can. I'm so freaked out I don't know if I'll ever sleep. I keep seeing things out of the corners of my eyes. A picture fell off the wall in the living room after you left. Are you sure there are no ghosts here?"

"There are ghosts; they just aren't going to talk to you today," Natasha said patiently.

"But why? What does it matter?"

"It just does." Natasha yawned. "Now try to get some sleep."

Madeline stood up hesitantly. She looked at Natasha and started to say something but stopped herself. "Okay. I'm going," she said. "Goodnight."

"Goodnight."

No sooner had Madeline left the room than Edwin returned, raging with lust. He pushed Natasha back onto the bed and slammed into her repeatedly. She muffled her cries into the pillow as he turned her over and pumped her doggy-style. His immense ghost cock was bigger than any cock, living or dead, she'd ever felt. With the pain came a sudden burst of pleasure. The pushing and pulling of her pussy caused her to gasp and moan, and her legs shook as she tried to keep her balance. Her face was pushed farther into the pillows as he held her hips, fucking her harder and faster until he came with a loud, moaning howl.

The door flew open, and Natasha scrambled under the bedclothes.

"What the fuck was that?" Madeline cried as she ran over to Natasha. "What?"

"Didn't you hear it? That horrible wailing?"

Natasha nodded as she clicked on the light once more. "Yes, I heard it too."

"My God, Natasha. I've never been so freaked out in my life. Can I sleep here with you?"

Natasha nodded, and the heated room turned cool once again. "Yes, you can sleep with me," she said as Madeline climbed under the covers with her.

"I'm freaking," Madeline said.

"It's okay," Natasha replied. "Nothing is going to harm you. I promise."

Madeline whimpered as Natasha stroked her hair. From downstairs, there was crashing sound of dishes being broken.

"There's going to be some mess to clean up tomorrow," Natasha tried to joke.

"I'm not even going to go down to look. Not 'til morning, anyway," Madeline said. "It's okay. We'll come back with a team. I'm sure next time will be better for you,"

Natasha said. "Now go to sleep."

She snuggled in beside Madeline and held the shivering girl until her breathing became more regular. At last, she was asleep.

Natasha turned off the light and quickly fell asleep herself.

The next time they came to the house, things would be different. Edwin's satisfied presence in the corner assured her of that.

In the meantime, her hunger grew.

Chapter Six

Get out and meet new people.

Natasha and Maggie Go Cruising

"I thought you had a new boyfriend," Natasha said as Maggie slid into the seat across from her. Maggie's exuberance was spilling from her as she shrugged off her coat in the small wooden chair.

"He's really a great guy," Maggie said as she reached for a menu.

"I told you," Natasha replied, tipping a glass of red wine toward herself. "He's the one.""I don't know why," Maggie said. "There's something there. And he's so passionate.""Who would have thought?" Natasha smirked. "Didn't I tell you? Not everyone jumps into bed on the first date."

"I know. I always knew that. But I'm good now," Maggie said and turned her attention to the waitress who came over to take her order.

"A pint of Amber Brew," she said. The waitress nodded and bopped away in time to the beat of the old Stones song that vibrated through the bar.

Natasha sighed.

"So if he's so great, why are you out here with me?" Natasha asked.

"He's going to play darts with some friends, and, quite frankly, I'm not so big on the darts," Maggie said.

"I can understand that." Natasha winked and watched a conversation unfolding at the bar. She couldn't hear what was being said, but a foggy mist settled over the top of the men and hovered. When she was younger, she thought such mists were the cigarette smoke that hung thick in the air before the no-smoking laws took effect. However, long after smoking was banned in public places, she was still able to see thick puffs of smoke hovering above people.

The smoke or mist was nothing to be feared. It was the watchful souls of those who had passed on yearning to send messages to their loved ones.

Natasha could focus on them one at a time and understand what they were trying to say. She'd learned long ago not to pass along the messages unless it was in a controlled setting.

The results were too unpredictable.

So while Maggie prattled on about her clients at the flea market, Natasha watched as the blond man's grandmother tried to get his attention to tell him about the hidden deed in the barn. At times like this, Natasha yearned to march over to the person and tell him about the message, especially when it was so obviously needed, judging by the way the young man dressed.

But in the past, when Natasha had tried to pass along such messages, there had been problems.

The last thing she needed was more problems.

"Who was that guy you were dancing with all night

on New Year's Eve?" Maggie asked. Natasha jerked her attention back to Maggie.

"I'm sorry," Natasha said. "'The guy'? Gus? I introduced you."

"No. I mean where did you meet? You never did say. You came together.""No, I didn't." Natasha smiled. "And now is not the time to tell the story.""Now I'm really intrigued," Maggie said. "Tell me."

"Shh." Natasha put a finger to her lips. Her smile was secretive as she shook her head slowly. "Not now."

Maggie's beer came, and their chatter turned to the men in the room.

"Those two guys at the bar look lonely. Let's go talk to them," Maggie said as she drained the last of her beer.

"Maggie. You like Weldon, remember?" Natasha scolded mockingly.

"I can talk to other guys, can't I? I would expect him to talk to other girls."

"Honestly?" Natasha raised an eyebrow.

"Why not?" Maggie said as she waved at the waitress to bring another round. "No harm in talking."

Natasha followed her over to the bar, and before long, they were engulfed in conversation

The blond guy, Pete, drank his beer nonchalantly, unaware of his grandmother's frantic, eternal wailing for his attention just above his head. The granny's shrieks seared through Natasha's head, and she could barely hear Pete's question.

"I'm Natasha," she said coolly, sticking out her hand. "I know you're Pete and that your grandmother loved you."

"No shit," Pete said.

"Well, your friend told me your name."

"No, my grandma. She died about three months ago."

"Were you close?"

"Yeah, I lived with her since I was three."

"Here in Hermana?"

"Yeah, just on the outskirts of town."

"The old Jessop place?"

"That's the one."

Natasha looked above him once more.

"Do you believe in ghosts?" she asked. The deeper she fell into connection with Granny, the hungrier she became. Her teeth itched, and her gaze fell from the swirling cloud above him to the throbbing vein his neck. She licked her lips and returned her dark-eyed gaze to his blue one.

"I sometimes think she's around," he said. "I wouldn't say that if I wasn't in this town, if you know what I mean."

"Sure." She nodded, wishing the gnawing rumble in her stomach would go away. "Natasha," Maggie said, "do you want to go dancing at the Cave?"

"Right now?" Natasha said.

"It's not that late," Maggie said. "And no work in the morning for either of us. Heck, I pity those who do have to work, the way the snow's been coming down."

"Well, I guess," Natasha said, hoping the Cave would prove a distraction for another night before she'd have to feed again.

* * *

The night went well, and the boys danced with the girls until the lights came on. Natasha was relieved that between the loud music and the dancing, Granny didn't have the energy to hang around.

As everyone piled on layers of clothes at the coat check, Maggie impulsively kissed Tom on the cheek.

"Goodnight."

Natasha gave her a steely-eyed stare. Once they were far enough down the sidewalk from the men, Natasha playfully punched Maggie in the arm.

"What were you thinking? Kissing him like that?"

"What? It was a goodnight kiss. So what?"

"So, you like this Weldon guy?" Natasha said sarcastically.

"So?"

"You've had sex with Weldon."

"Again, so what?"

"You know what I'm trying to say."

"Christ, Natasha, I didn't fuck him. I kissed him goodnight. I do that to lots of people, including you."

"It was more than a kiss. You didn't fuck him in the bathroom, did you?"

"No."

Natasha stared at her. "I hope not. Weldon's a good guy. Give him a chance. Jeez, you'd think you'd last a month!"

"Hey, he's the one who went out with his buddies."

"And he probably really is playing darts and shooting the shit with his buddies, not dirty-dancing with some girl he barely knows."

"So, I'm bad." Maggie sighed guiltily.

"I wouldn't love you if you weren't bad." Natasha laughed. "Just be careful. And give it a chance."

"I'll listen."

The women walked on in silence until they reached Maggie's building. They hugged and kissed each other goodnight. She climbed the huge stone staircase as Natasha continued down the street in silence.

The snow was falling in thick clumps, and she was glad she wore heavy hiking boots while carrying her shoes in a leather knapsack.

As she turned down the dark, narrow street toward her home, she was aware of footsteps behind her. She knew not to be afraid as she turned around.

"Pete," she said, staring at the young man who had a floating mist above his head. "You startled me."

"Sorry about that. "

"What are you doing? Are you following me?" she asked. The cloud swarm grew larger above his head, and soon Natasha was hypnotized by the shrieking chaos from within.

"Yes, I had to know about what you said.""What did I say?"

"About my grandmother. It's like she's here now and I have to talk to you."

A wave of relief swept through Natasha. She held out her mittened hands to Pete's gloved ones.

As their fingers linked, the granny's shrieks flooded through both of them. Peter jolted back.

"Stop yelling," Natasha said. "I can hear you." The wailing stopped. Natasha smiled. "Okay, we're listening."

Pete cocked his head. "I can't hear anything."

"It's okay. I can." Natasha listened as Granny gave careful instructions on how Pete was to find the deed. As Natasha started to relay the message, Pete's eyes grew wide.

"How do you know these things? Have you been there?"

"No, she's telling me." Natasha continued with the details, and Pete listened in silence. At last, his grandmother was finished with her message and dissolved happily back into nothing.

"Wow, that was intense. She's gone now, right?" Pete said. "Yes. What did you experience?"

"Just feelings. I couldn't hear her like you could, but I could feel her. "

"Yes, feeling is part of it. One day the voices come to some of us. Not the best gift to have, but not the worst either."

The hunger in her swelled, and she was glad they were dressed so heavily.

"I gotta go. Thanks, Natasha!" Pete bounded off down the street. Natasha walked on and listened as his footsteps faded. There was little sound from the streets save the humming of electrical wires. Not many people favored being out in snow like this.

As Natasha continued on, there was the distant roar like that of a wild animal and a muffled shriek, and then all was still again. Probably a wolf getting a rabbit, she thought, but something inside her said it wasn't so.

Chapter Seven

Be careful and don't take foolish chances.

Hunger

The hunger was strong that day. From the moment she had awakened, it was clear the piddly sips here and there weren't going to appease her much longer. It was time for a road trip.

Natasha threw a suitcase into the car and drove into Boston. After she checked into the cheapest chain hotel she could find, she changed into a black PVC catsuit with thigh-high boots and elbow-length gloves. She looped chains around her narrow waist and hooked a small, black flogger to one of them. Large quantities of charcoal around her eyes and giant fake eyelashes gave her a dangerous look. As she painted her lips burgundy, she hoped the club would be busy.

Before she left, she covered the bed with several sets of large, old towels she had brought from home.

Her wish was granted as she walked down the stairs toward glass doors. The vibration of the music through her stiletto boots filled her with anticipation. She paid the cover charge, checked her coat and entered the club. It was as she remembered it from her last visit a few months earlier. The entrance emptied into one large room where there was a full-sized stage, a bar and a giant dance floor already full of gyrating, leather-clad bodies. Lit doorways reassured her that the playrooms were open.

Natasha bought a drink at the bar and stood taking in the scene around her. Pieces of equipment were against the walls. Around the room, people were playing on a spank table, a bench, an electric chair and other similar devices.

The steady smacking of leather against bare asses blended with the heavy-bass techno music. Natasha sipped her beer and walked on, grinning at the stares she received from men and women alike.

A shadow flitted across of the corner of her eye. She turned her head and spotted a man walking away from her down the hall. A tingle swept through her. That sickening sense of unease rushed back and then was gone just as quickly.

Coolly, she walked down one of the hallways, where several small rooms branched off on either side. The first room was empty. A woman in the second room was kneeling on a mattress, giving a man a blowjob. The third had a medical table where several people poked and prodded a naked, handcuffed girl.

The fourth room caught her attention. It was a bit bigger, and inside there was a big X. A man was shackled, wrist and ankle, to all four arms of the construction. Two women took turns flogging him. One wore leather shorts and a leather bra. The other wore a PVC corset and a tiny PVC skirt. Both ladies wore fishnets and tall platform shoes. Another couple sat to the side watching the scene.

Natasha knew the couple, though physically sitting together, wasn't together emotionally. He was a loner. His gaze shifted from the scene and toward her. His lost, lonely eyes told her that he was the one.

She carefully made her way past the flogging girls and sat down beside the man. As she watched the flogging continue, he spoke.

"Lovely evening for a flogging, isn't it?" he asked with a grin. Natasha smiled widely.

"It most certainly is." The man stood up so she could fully appreciate him. He wore a leather skirt, a slave collar and large leather wrist shackles. Silver buckles and D-rings glinted in the light. A long, heavy chain hung down his neck.

"You're a slave," she said simply as she touched his chain. He nodded, eyes wide with expectation.

"You need a mistress?" she asked while wrapping her fingers around the iron loops.

"Yes, I do."

"Obey me, then," she said as she tightened her grip and pulled him down until he was kneeling on the floor. "A slave must ask his mistress nicely and politely."

The man lowered his face to the floor.

"Please, will you be my mistress?" he asked. She put one stiletto boot on top of his head and pressed down with the ball of her foot.

"Pardon me? I didn't hear you the first time."

His words were muffled as he asked again. She admired the firm ripples of his lean back and the Y that led to his shapely ass hugged in leather, rising higher in the air the farther down she pushed. She unlocked the flogger from her belt.

"Stay there," she commanded as she took her foot from his head. As she walked around him, the woman he had been sitting with left. Natasha stood behind him and hit his butt with the flogger.

"Will you be my mistress?" he shouted.

"Pardon me?" she asked as she struck him again.

"Please, will you be my mistress?" The flogger struck once more. Natasha returned to stand in front of him..

"You may rise, and yes, I will accept you as my slave." Natasha took hold of the chain around his neck. He started to stand up.

"No, you may crawl behind me. I need to go to the bar for another drink, and you must come."

She led him around the crowded dance floor and up to the bar. She picked a stool to sit on as she ordered another beer. The man lay on the floor beside the stool.

Her blood was racing. Her hands shook as she brought the drink to her mouth. She had to do it soon or she would pass out and who knew where that would be? She shuddered to think of it. The dancers distracted her as the music calmed her for a few moments more.

The shuddering began. had begun. It crept through her fingers and down to her wrists. Tiny tremors that signified that bigger things were on the way. Still, if she didn't handle the situation perfectly she would lose a pretty sure bet.

He was more pleasant than a passed-out drunk. She looked down at him, seeing past the bare flesh of his back, under his skin to the veins pulsing . Their steady throbbing beckoned her.

Must remain cool.

Once she finished her drink, Natasha stood up, tugging on the leash. Slave followed. More people had come in, and it was getting hard to walk around with him on all fours. She led him into the corner of one of the rooms, where a schoolgirl was whipping a half-naked nun over a desk. The room was set up like a classroom, and "I will not be a dirty nun" was written on the chalkboard.

"This place is really crowded," Natasha said. "Do you want to take this somewhere else?"

"Where? I can't go to my place…"

"It's okay. I have a hotel room. We'll go there."

"Are you sure?" he asked. "You don't know me."

"You don't know me, either." She winked. "What do you say?"

"Sure thing. I have to get dressed first."

Natasha laughed. "I'll wait by the dance floor."

As she stood watching the bodies writhe before her, she wondered what he'd taste like.

He knelt naked before her. Natasha still wore her catsuit. His nakedness was as appealing as his outfit had been. She smiled as she sized him up.

"You may look at me," she said throatily. He stared up at her. She slowly unzipped the front of her catsuit. She unpeeled it from her body as his erection bobbed in appreciation.

"You here for a good time?" she asked, standing naked in front of him.

"Whatever you desire, mistress."

"Good, get on the bed." She pointed and he complied. Her hand wavered and she quickly lowered it, hoping he didn't notice the shivers passing through her body at an alarming rate. "I can't wait," she said as she took his penis into her mouth.

"I...I'm married, you know. I can't let my wife find out about this," he stammered. "I'm not telling anyone. I'm not even from around here. Just passing through on business."

She winked and returned to sucking him. He leaned back, comforted by her words, comforted more by her warm lips working their magic on his cock.

When he was fully hard, she slid onto him and wasted no time building up to a steady, firm rhythm. His hips rose to meet her, and she leaned over to suckle his nipples. She quickly made her way up to his neck, grinding harder against him in anticipation. The tremors shook her as she sank her teeth into his neck. Welcome relief swelled through her as the blood gushed into her mouth and her pussy throbbed with her orgasm.

He continued to fuck her until the pain of her drinking took over.

"Whoa now, you're too rough," he said, trying to push her up. Her grip on him from pussy to mouth was strong, and he was pinned beneath her. She clamped a hand over his mouth, and though he struggled, she was too much for him. Her noisy slurps filled the room until he lapsed into unconsciousness.

Natasha finally stopped her feast and pushed a rolled-up towel against his neck to stop the bleeding. Belly bloated, she stood up and wiped her mouth with the back of her hand. She staggered to the bathroom. When she looked in the mirror, she saw a face that was blood-smeared but rejuvenated. The sallow hollows around her eyes had already filled in, and her cheeks were more flushed by the minute. She would enjoy her rosy glow for a few hours until her natural paleness returned.

The shower was warm and inviting as she lathered bubbles through her long, dark hair and along her narrow waist. Blood swirled down the drain, lost in the labyrinth of soap and water. When the water finally ran clear, she stepped out. She toweled dry and returned to the bedroom naked.

Slave lay on the bed. The formerly white towel was now crimson. She went over to him and felt his pulse. Still alive. She took away the towel and put it in a bag. She brought several more old towels out of her suitcase. Packing his wound tightly, Natasha hoped he'd stop bleeding.

The television was too soft to hear, so she turned it up and idly clicked the remote until she found an old sitcom. After an hour, she checked the towels. The wound was clotting.

Natasha put the towels in the bag with the other towel and packed them in her suitcase. She found her first aid kit and cleaned out his wound. He was so far gone that he didn't even wince. Once the wound was cleaned, she was pleased to see that he looked pretty normal, even if he was extraordinarily pale. There was no sign of blood anywhere else.

She stood at the door and looked into the room as if she were discovering him for the first time. At first, he was a man asleep. Naked with a limp dick. Nice cherubic face and muscular chest. Only when she got closer could she see that his pallor was strange. Since his head was slightly cocked, the wounds weren't visible at all.

85

It would work fine.

She packed up her belongings and changed into jeans.

"Good-bye and thank you," she said as she clicked off the light. Slave said nothing in the glow of the television.

Natasha drove back to Hermana and arrived home just before the first light of dawn.

Chapter Eight

Spend the day with those you love.

Natasha's Birthday

When Natasha woke, the moon was just starting to drift into the sky. The last glowing fingers of the sun stretched over Hermana's main street and glimmered on the water by the beach. The snow sparkled as the twinning powers of sun and moon touched and retreated toward their respective paths. She glanced at the clock. Only an hour before circle at Lucy's.

She tossed her covers aside and made her way to the bathroom. As she shucked her floor-length, white nightgown, her flesh prickled with the cool air.

Drafty, she thought as she stepped into the clawfoot tub and turned on the shower. She pulled the sheer, white cloth curtain around the tub. The spray was shockingly cold at first but grew warmer as it steadily pounded against her. Her thoughts drifted as warm steam filled the chilly bathroom.

Funny how her birthday fell on a full moon this year. It was especially auspicious that Lucy's circle was taking place this night as well. Some months, she faced the circle of her peers with trepidation. She was leery of how much about her they could figure out with their own magical powers. She knew some of the ladies were creeped out by her dark eyes and ageless face. Especially as theirs grew older with lines and jowls.

She had lost track of her birthdays, although she knew she must be hitting another century soon.

One time, decades, maybe even a century ago— she would have to reread her journal again—she had gone to a fortune-teller while living in Spain. It had been a damp, chilly night and the caravans all had little fires in front of them. Natasha had heard tales of Savanna but wanted to see for herself if all that was said was true.

Savanna was easy enough to find. She looked to be in her forties although legend had it that she was much older. She knew about many types of spells and remedies. Natasha asked her if she could heal blood cravings.

Savanna laughed, her dark eyes flashing in the firelight as glittering bells tinkled on the edges of the many scarves she wore.

"No, my dear. I'm sorry." Her voice was boisterous yet worn. "The call of the blood is one curse I can't destroy. I don't think anyone can."

"I didn't think so." Natasha stared into the fire for a moment. "But there's another spell I've heard that you do."

"Now, which one would that be? You'd be amazed at what I can do."

"Well, it's a memory thing. For those with eternal life," Natasha said.

"Yes, the memory-fragment spell. Do you want to know how it works?"

"Of course."

"Very well. The spell erases the memory so you're only allowed to think back 50 years, give or take. That way, you don't lament all those whom you've loved and lost, but conversely, you can't learn from past mistakes, either."

"There's always a catch."

Savanna nodded. "I've done it. That's why I write everything down. My wagon is filled with spells and journals of important ideas I don't want to forget."

"And you don't regret it."

"There's always regret, my dear. It's the human condition." She stood up abruptly and led Natasha inside.

That was all Natasha remembered anymore. Soon, she would forget the lady had erased her memory at all, but she had written it down and made herself read the journals periodically to remember who she was.

Natasha soaped up her long, lean body, admiring how smooth and soft her skin was on this finest of days. She thought about her good friends who would be at the circle and how happy they would be to celebrate her birthday with her.

A gust of cold air blew the curtain, and, for a moment, Natasha caught a glimpse of a man standing there. A terrible-looking wreck of a man with blood smeared from head to toe.

"Who's there?" Natasha asked as she cocked her head, trying to listen to the spirit. She wasn't able to hear him and gasped as she saw the imprint of his face pressing against the shower curtain. Instinctively she covered herself.

"Who are you?" she said firmly. "Name yourself."

"You know who I am. I course through your veins."

The face disappeared as did the coldness, and Natasha turned back to the shower. One of her victims coming to bitch at her.

But from when, she had no idea.

Natasha continued to wash and think about the circle until she realized she'd better just plain get there.

When she opened the door to leave her loft, she was stunned by a very large bouquet of black roses in a crystal vase in the hallway. She plucked the card from the holder and grinned as she read it.

Happy Birthday, Natasha
Your new friend, Gus

So Gus was thinking about her all this time. She just hadn't been able to find him, yet he knew where she lived. She wondered if he had delivered the flowers himself, knocking on her door while she slept her fitful sleep.

It was a shame she hadn't seen him. She didn't even know how to get in touch to thank him.

She put the flowers on the dining table, spent a moment admiring how well they suited her decor and set out for the circle.

A while later, she was walking through the snowy streets toward Lucy's house on the other side of the beach. She knew she would be late, but no matter how late she was, someone, likely Maggie, would be later.

The house was immense and beautiful in an old New England mansion sort of way. There were turrets and large paneled windows. Unlike modern, boxy houses, this structure had many rooms with bay windows protruding from all sides.

In all the years she had known Lucy, Natasha had never been up into the attic. In fact, she was certain there were many areas of Lucy's home she'd never seen. Lucy probably barely used them as she was getting on in years herself. However, unlike Natasha, Lucy was mortal and wanted to stay mortal. As much magic as Lucy conjured, she had always been fearful of eternal life and its consequences.

Natasha didn't know if Lucy knew what she was, and if she did, she never let on. Natasha noted the many footprints in the snow leading up the grand granite stairs at the front entrance. Lucy loved art, and everywhere Natasha looked, there were sculptures and sconces of gargoyles and other winged creatures.

A chill ran up her back, and she looked behind her to see if someone was following her. It was almost a way of life, turning around to see if someone was trying to get to her, living or dead.

She entered the giant ornate lobby and handed her coat to one of the uniformed servants. Lucy's money was old and invested in the town. As much as Lucy enjoyed an opulent lifestyle, she also enjoyed sharing her good fortune with others.

Most of the other ladies were in the circle room when Natasha arrived. She hugged and kissed Madeline and Veronica, then turned to Ellie.

"Maggie's not here yet, I see."

"No, as late as you are, you still beat her." Ellie giggled.

"Good."

"Happy birthday," Ellie said as she hugged Natasha. "I'm sure we'll be celebrating later."

Gwen and Ursula came over to give their birthday greetings to Natasha. "How old are you now?" Ursula said as she reached up to kiss Natasha.

"Can't be a day over 30, except that I've known you for about ten years," Toni joked as she squeezed Ursula and Natasha in her arms. "Happy birthday, darling." Toni tossed her short, black hair.

"Oh, you cut it all off," Natasha said as she lightly touched it. "How '20's. You look like a flapper."

"You like it?" Toni turned around. "I heard it was all the rage."

"In the Roaring Twenties." Gwen laughed.

"Oh my God, Gwen. You made it. In this weather." Natasha hugged Gwen. "It must have taken forever."

"Well, it was a good two hours from the Boston airport, but I'm here now. Ready to use your birthday greetings to bring love into my life."

"Boy, do I need some good-year bumping," Lily said, joining the group. "It's been forever."

"Dry spells all around," Toni said.

"Not Maggie. She's the first to go in a long time," Ellie said conspiratorially.

"Oh yeah. That guy she was all over New Year's Eve. Well, you know Maggie, he won't last long." said Toni.

"I don't know. She's rather smitten," Natasha said.

"I guess it's going well. From all accounts. Well, she can tell you herself if she ever gets here," Ellie said as she looked toward the lobby.

"Maggie in love. Wow." Toni sighed. "So romantic. Right on the new year."

"Yeah. Amazing, isn't it?" Ellie said.

"Ellie *feng shui*ed her house according to Gwen's astrology charts," Natasha told them. "I think that and the circle brought love into her life."

"You don't say." Veronica tossed her hair and put her arms around Toni and Ursula. "Maybe we should all do that. On our birthdays, we *feng shui*, do a circle and see what happens."

"I'm one step ahead of you." Natasha laughed. "Ellie just did my music room. And I think it's working already."

"Not that guy from the jazz band?" Ellie said.

"What guy from the jazz band? I thought she was getting hot and bothered on New Year's Eve with that Gus guy," Toni said, cocking her head at Natasha.

Natasha grinned. "Gus did send me flowers for my birthday. Black roses."

"Get out," Ursula said.

"Perfect for the music room," Ellie said. "Put them in your love corner."

"I'll remember that," Natasha said.

"Maybe it's the beginning of a magical year." Toni grinned. "Wouldn't that be romantic?"

"Wouldn't it be great to fall in love?" Veronica sighed.

"I want to know how Natasha keeps having

birthdays and looks younger each year." Ursula wagged her finger at Natasha.

"One day she'll share with us the secret to her eternal youth." Toni winked. "That new Botox clinic, perhaps? I've been there myself."

Natasha smiled secretly and let them rib her.

At last, Maggie bustled into the room, all scattered energy as she begged forgiveness for being late yet again. The women quickly greeted her as the sweet smell of burning frankincense filled the room from wrought-iron pots swinging from chains on large posts at the far end of the room beside a large carved throne.

The center of the room was carpeted with a deep black runner. The spots in the circle were well worn where some of the ladies had stood for years. Lucy was wealthy partly because she was thrifty. The carpet had been in the house for over a hundred years.

Lucy entered the room wearing a long, black robe. She stood at the front, near her mammoth throne, and greeted the ladies.

"Good evening, everyone. Welcome to the first full moon circle of the year. And for double good blessings, today is Natasha's birthday."

The ladies politely clapped as Natasha blushed.

"Tonight, we're going to focus on bringing in positive energy for the new year. New loves, new beginnings, new jobs, new clients."

The ladies murmured happily among themselves.

"You may find this will be a difficult year for some of you and yet for others, a prosperous one. You must remember to consult your charts or, if you can't do it, get someone like Gwen to prepare one for you.

The planetary alignments are very important in your lives, as you've grown to understand. This is why we cast our circles on full moons or new moons or special occasions such as the solstice. But enough of that. Put on your robes and we shall begin."

The ladies made their way over to the four cloaked handmaidens who had their robes sorted and ready for them. Each lady stripped off her clothes, folding them neatly and putting them on the large wooden shelves that covered one entire side of the room. The clothes didn't take up much space. Other shelves were filled with books, jars of liquid, herbs and other ingredients for spells.

Once naked, Natasha slid the robe over her body, pulling the hood over her hair.

Thick incense burned in the air as Lucy rang a small bell. Candles flickered from sconces in the walls and along the altars that ran along the other side of the room.

The 12 women stood in their places in the circle.

Lucy stepped into the center of the circle with a large bowl of salt. She scooped up a handful and walked around in front of the women until she had made a complete circle. When she was done, she returned the bowl to the nearest altar and took her place with the others.

Natasha could feel the energy shifting as the ladies focused into the circle. She closed her eyes and followed along as Lucy led them through a full moon ritual. They hummed and chanted, holding hands, lighting candles and willing themselves to become something better than what they were.

Natasha thought about Gus and wondered what

he was doing that night. It would have been nice to spend her birthday with him.

"Natasha, what wishes do you have for the coming year?" Lucy's voice broke into her thoughts. Lucy opened her eyes and looked at the ladies watching her.

"I want to understand myself better. I want to learn how to control my gifts in a way that will serve my sisters."

Lucy nodded. "Let the spirits of the gods and goddess, the spirit mother-father and the elements of earth, wind, fire and water guide Natasha in her quest for knowledge and truth."

"Blessed be," the ladies chorused.

"What else do you desire on this most auspicious of days?" Lucy asked her.

Natasha closed her eyes and thought about Gus and the black roses. She was intrigued. "I want to meet my soul mate. My lover, my companion; someone to share in the darkness and light."

"I think that sounds like something everyone in this room desires, doesn't it?" Lucy said. "Who doesn't want to meet her soul mate? So many of you ladies have been single far too long. It's time to get a companion to share your life with."

Toni opened her mouth to say something and then stopped. Lucy turned to her. "Toni? You have something to say?"

Toni shrugged. "I don't know if I want to be tied down. I like having lots of guys."

"Spoken like an Aries. That's okay, Toni. When it's your soul mate, your true soul mate, you're not tied down. You're complemented."

"I don't know." Toni sighed.

"No, you don't. But you will. And you will find it refreshing. Trust me on that," Lucy said.

"How do you know? When were you ever married?" asked Toni.

Lucy sighed. "I've loved and lost. Yes, too many times. I'm a private person, and my affairs happened long before any of you were even born. Well, almost all of you," she said, staring at Natasha, who looked at the floor. "I didn't give up on love, but instead, I fueled my fantasies into a higher power. I use my energy for you ladies, to help you live fruitful, productive lives and empower your gifts."

"I see," Toni said.

"But enough of that. Let's get back to work. Everyone, breathe deeply and focus on opening your heart and mind to bring love into your life."

When the circle was finished, Natasha breathed a sigh of relief. The energy had been so high and Lucy had made that little public jab at her. Well, she couldn't really blame her. Lucy had been around as far back as she could remember, and likely farther back still. Lucy had always been in her life.

After the circle, the ladies had wine and a buffet with chicken breasts for the carnivores and falafels for the vegetarians. They drank wine and toasted Natasha's birthday.

Natasha noticed Lucy was staring at her. Lucy waved her hand, motioning for her to come over.

As Lucy led her down the hall, she spoke excitedly. "I have something to give you, Natasha. Follow me."

They arrived at one of the many bedrooms in the

west wing, and Lucy went to a jewelry box on the dresser. She held up a large golden locket. The stone in it was a large opal with diamonds around the edges in the gold facing. The oval-shaped locket was as big as Natasha's palm. The heavy gold chain was braided and doubled to hold the weight of the stone.

"Here, you need to have this," Lucy said as she placed it in Natasha's hand. The locket was cool and heavy, a pleasant vibration emanating from it.

"What is it?" Natasha asked. "It's beautiful." She held up the locket to study it better. The diamonds sparkled, and the opal glittered with secrets.

"It belonged to Sorona herself," Lucy whispered, her eyes dancing. Natasha stared at her, incredulous.

"But why?" she asked. "Why me? I'm not family."

Lucy held one of Natasha's hands and looked her directly in the eye. "There may come a time when I'm not going to be here. You and I both know that no one lives forever." Natasha swallowed. Lucy continued on. "I don't know if you'll live forever, if anyone can. Surely, the body wears out no matter how many spells you do. I don't know. I just know I'm mortal and I can feel my body crumbling."

"Oh, Lucy." Natasha sighed. "You—"

Lucy raised her hand as she spoke. "No. It's part of old age, and I accept it. I'm not afraid to finish my job on this earth and move on. I know there are better things waiting for me. My family waits for me. Sorona and Serephena are waiting to meet me." She smiled, her well-worn face glowing, her eyes distant to the heavens. She took a deep breath and turned back to Natasha, her eyes flashing once more. "But I do know you've got a secret;

you'll be here long after I'm gone. I'm giving this to you on the promise you'll lead the circle when I go or at least until you can find someone really willing to be there for the long haul."

Natasha rubbed the stone. It buzzed warmly and comfortingly under her fingers. Lucy's request had caught her off guard.

"But shouldn't there be a relative?" Natasha asked. "A relative to continue on the work of Sorona and Serephena?"

"I trust you more. You have been here every circle…for decades. You know how it's done, how to calm the ladies. You know what to do."

"I do." Natasha nodded. "Thank you, Lucy, for trusting me with this precious gift. I won't let you down."

Natasha hugged Lucy. The tiny, frail woman was so delicate in her arms. Natasha sometimes wondered why she didn't just blow away in the wind. Lucy wrapped her arms around Natasha, her tiny arms barely meeting as she rubbed Natasha's back. The energy from Lucy was warm and plaintive but calming.

When Natasha pulled away, Lucy had tears in her eyes.

"Oh, Natasha. Be careful." Lucy clutched Natasha's arms.

Natasha looked at her quizzically. "Be careful of what?"

"I'm not sure. There's some bad energy around you, and I don't want to see you get hurt. Wear it always." Lucy touched the amulet that was still in Natasha's hand.

"I will," Natasha said as she hung the locket around her neck. It was heavy, but it felt natural, as though it should have always been there.

"Don't you look regal?" Lucy smiled. "Welcome to the family. And happy birthday."

When Natasha returned to the room, the ladies were huddled around in a circle, whispering.. The energy was sharp and tumultuous as she approached them.

"What is it?" she asked.

"Did you hear?" Maggie asked. "That's why I was late. I just saw it on television."

"Hear what?" Natasha asked impatiently. She could tell by the long look on Ellie's face that she wasn't going to like what she was going to hear.

"That guy, Pete. He's dead."

Natasha stared at Maggie. "That Pete guy? From the Cave?"

"Yeah. They found him all torn up. Like a wild animal got him," Maggie said, her eyes welling up with tears.

"Maybe a wolf? Or bear even?" Toni said.

"That's crazy," Natasha said.

"I feel so bad about it," Maggie said. "I was trying to be all fun when I came in so I wouldn't ruin the circle. But now…well, shit."

"I know. It's just so bizarre." Natasha pulled Maggie aside to talk alone. "You know, he ran after me. I had told him some stuff about his grandmother and he wanted to know more, so I told him. After he left, I thought I heard a noise."

"What kind of noise?" Maggie's eyes were wide.

"I don't know. A scream. A wild animal,"

Natasha said. "I didn't really think anything of it. Sounds of the night in New England. Could have even be cats fighting. Who knows?"

"But it was Pete. Getting attacked."

Natasha shook her head. "Now I feel bad. I wonder if I could have done anything."

"Just be grateful it wasn't you," Maggie said. "What else could you have done? It was his time."

The women hugged one another. From the other room, the rest of the women were calling for Natasha. When she returned, a large birthday cake complete with lit candles and her name written in fancy frosting script greeted her.

Natasha touched her amulet, made a wish, then blew out each and every candle.

Chapter Nine

Listen to the music within yourself.

Music Has Charm

Natasha ran her bow along the strings as the brightness of the full moon cast a spotlight on her. Craig plucked his guitar, and as they played together the cacophony of sound was discordant and catchy.

When the song came to an end, Natasha put down her violin and bow. "I'm thirsty," she said. "I'll go get some wine."

"Do you have beer?" Craig asked as he placed his guitar in the stand.

"Beer it is," Natasha said as she went through the door to her apartment. As she pulled on the door, she was aware of the energy shift.

They had been waiting for her, listening at the door, seething with impatience as the recent smudging kept them at bay.

They swirled feverishly around her as Natasha pulled two beers out of the fridge. She batted at them as if they were pesky flies. Their misty forms twirled around her head, their anguish making her dizzy. They chattered and chided at her, resentful of being locked out of her room.

"On second thought," she said as she pulled out two more, "don't want to come back in here if I don't have to."

She took the beers and the opener back into the other room. The ghosts teased her hair and pulled at her clothes, urging her to come back and be with them.

"Bye-bye," she said as she kicked the door shut.

"Huh?" Craig asked, looking up from a music book.

"Sorry. Just talking to myself."

Craig laughed. "I do that too. A sign of genius, or maybe it's just insanity."

Natasha put the beer down on the coffee table. "I brought several so I don't have to keep going back and forth. Help yourself." She gestured at them.

Craig opened a beer and gave it to her. He opened another one and took a long swig from it. "Ah, that's better," he said. "I'm much better now."

"Me too," Natasha said. "Beer was a good idea."

The smell of his cologne was sweet; his sweat was sweeter. Natasha's teeth began to itch. She took another sip of beer. She couldn't start getting hungry again so soon. She had to wait.

Craig continued to talk about the merits of beer while Natasha stared at his neck. The veins throbbed when he talked, enticing her. Up and down, undulating blood flowed through them. Rich, red blood that tasted so wonderfully salty. She could almost taste it oozing along her tongue, dripping down her throat.

Natasha drank the rest of her beer in one gulp. A burp slipped from her lips, surprising her. Embarrassed, she clapped her hands over her mouth.

103

"Oh my goodness. I'm so sorry," she said, her face growing flushed. "I never—"

"That's what happens when you drink beer fast, little lady," Craig drawled. "You'll be belching like the men folk 'round here."

They laughed as he opened another beer for her. As he handed it to her, he teased, "Now you drive slower this time, hear?"

"Righty so, pardner." Natasha lifted the beer and took a ladylike sip from it as proof. Before long, they decided to jam some more. They were learning how to feed off each other in a harmonious give-and-take that resulted in sensational vibrations resonating through the room. Natasha was lost in the reverie of their music when there was a crash outside the window.

Even Craig heard it through the sound of his wailing guitar. "What the fuck was that?" he asked as he clutched the neck of his guitar and held it out like a weapon.

"It sounded like something just outside the window." Natasha looked toward the window where the sound had originated.

"This high up?" Craig asked.

"Well, it could have been from the street. That window over there is open a bit to keep the air flow going."

"It sounded like someone was out there."

"I do have a fire escape," Natasha said. "One can't be too careful in these old places."

"That's it, then," Craig said as he ran toward the window. He lifted it up and looked down the fire escape. Natasha saw a dark figure loping down the street. She couldn't tell if it was a man running with his coat flapping or if it was a bear.

"There's nothing there," Craig said, satisfied he had looked down the fire escape enough. "Maybe it was just a raccoon. Look, that flower pot is broken."

"Yeah, I get raccoons a lot. He probably ran up to the roof," she said, looking up. He followed her gaze.

"I don't see him now. He's lucky this time," Craig said as he shut the window. "Do you mind? I don't want to see any raccoon running in here. Or anything else."

"Not at all," Natasha said, locking the window. After glancing at his face, she went around and locked all the windows, even ones that weren't near the fire escape.

"Better?" she asked.

"Almost," he said as he put his arms around her and pulled her toward him. He kissed her long and full on the lips. When he was done, he stepped back and stared into her eyes. "Now I'm better."

Natasha smiled coyly. "I can make you feel even better." She kneeled down and unbuckled his belt. Within seconds and with his help, she had his penis out. He sighed as she sucked him fully.

"Oh yes. You know how to make a man feel real good."

As Natasha sucked him, she wondered about the noise and the figure she had seen. She touched the locket around her neck. It felt warm. She wondered if that was a sign.

"Oh, deeper, baby. That's it, that's good," he directed her as she sucked him. When he was hard, she took a condom from her purse on the coffee table and slid it over him. She hiked up her skirt and leaned over the couch. He held her hips as he slid his cock into her warm, moist pussy.

"Yes." She sighed. "That's it." He pushed deeply into her and held it for a moment until they both could feel him throbbing with excitement inside her.

He pulled out slowly, then plunged himself in quickly and deeply, causing her to moan. "Oh, God, that's delicious," she sighed. "So good."

He teased her for a while, changing strokes and depths until his own excitement took hold. His fingers danced on her clit while he pushed into her rhythmically.

"Oh yes." She sighed. "Yes. Yes."

Just when she thought he was going to come, he pulled out. "Lie down," he panted. "I want to look at your face."

She lay down. He held her legs up as he entered her, staring into her eyes.

Natasha could see lust in his eyes and something more. A softness she hadn't seen in a long time.

He pulled out and thrust in again repeatedly. The smell of him so near caused her stomach to rumble with hunger and excitement. The flesh of his neck was so close, and it would be so easy to just have a nibble. A teeny, tiny taste.

She reached up, clamping her mouth over his neck. She sucked on his warm, salty flesh, her eyes rolling back in desire and anticipation. She didn't bite hard as he continued to fuck her.

"Oh, yes, baby," he cried out. "Nibble my neck, you sexy vampire. I love it."

She bit down harder, enough to taste a bit of salty blood. It stung her lips, her stomach roiling loudly as it craved more. She licked and sucked on his warm flesh, careful not to bite deeper, but carefully savoring the tiny, weeping wound. Her body quivered with excitement, and she was coming.

"Yes, come on my cock," he cried as he fucked her faster.

She held onto his neck as he pumped into her furiously. He came with a groan.

They lay together for a moment, and Natasha slowly released her mouth from his neck. She was frustrated but satiated at the same time. The little taste of him was delicious, but it only served to make her want more. His essence was sweet and hearty, much different from most of the married men she picked up at the fetish club. His flavor resembled virgins more than most of the men she had consumed over the years. Perhaps it was his innocence. Or maybe the sweetness was a result of his genuine affection for her.

Craig rolled off her, and they lay hanging off the couch for a bit. He touched his neck with his finger and saw a smudge of blood.

"You enjoy role-playing?" he asked, holding his finger up in the air to examine the smear of blood.

"I didn't hurt you, did I?" she asked, reaching over to his neck to wipe away the last drop of glistening blood with her fingers.

"Not at all. It was sexy. Delicious. Fun." He saw the blood on her fingers. "Although, you really did draw blood."

"I'm sorry," she said as she slowly licked her fingers. "It's a fetish, I guess."

"I like your fetish. We can play vampire anytime you like." Craig leaned over to kiss her. "Anytime at all."

Chapter Ten

You may run into an old friend.

The Flea Market

Natasha wandered through the mall's basement flea market. Psychics ran most of the booths from Hermana, although there was the usual collection of antique furniture and record dealers as well. Sometimes Natasha enjoyed looking through the posters of old movies and Broadway shows. Somewhere in the back recesses of her mind, dingy, dusty theaters and velvet seats danced in her fragmented memory. An old phonograph record was playing in one of the stalls as she flipped through the prints. It was the theme from *Limelight*, an old Charlie Chaplin movie.

The plaintive melody dredged up haunting sensations, as if she should remember something connected to the song but couldn't. She stared at an old Broadway poster for *Gypsy* and wondered if she had seen the show.

Around her, ghostly shapes took form and led each other through a slow and romantic dance. Natasha pretended she didn't see them, intensifying her mock search through the prints. Beside her, a little girl pointed to the ceiling and tugged at her mother.

"Look up there! They're dancing," she cried.

The mother looked up and shrugged. "There's nothing there, dear," she said and led the child away as she stared back to watch the couples embrace.

Natasha waited until the song ended, and then they were back again, pleading with her in their wailing grief to connect them with their loved ones. It was always worse at the flea market because so many objects belonged to those who had passed on.

Natasha put the prints back with a sigh and wandered farther down the aisles, halfheartedly looking at sweaters and T-shirts among the ornate antique jewelry.

At last, she was at Maggie's stall. Maggie sat at her little cloth-covered table, staring earnestly at her tarot cards while a young man sat expectantly in front of her.

"What does it say?" he asked. Natasha turned her attention from the tarot reading to the line of people waiting to see Maggie. Natasha wanted to tell her about Craig but there would be no talking to Maggie for a while. She continued on, her black boots carefully stepping along the cement floor that was slick with melted snow from people's boots.

Natasha reached her own booth, unlocked the padlock, slid back the gates and pulled open the drapes. She didn't come in on a regular basis because the work she did was better done at the client's house. Nevertheless, there were those curious enough to try to call dead loved ones in a mall, and it was her duty to help.

Once she had positioned her table and sign, she set to work dusting the glass counter that held many pieces of antique jewelry and tiny sculptures of musical instruments. She had a small rack of CDs by local artists who she enjoyed and tried to promote. She would have to remember to get Craig's band's CDs in there as well.

There were a few books on display too, written by various psychics who lived in Hermana. Most were small-press and self-published works, but the tourists seemed to enjoy them. They covered historical stories, orbs, ghosts, witches and witch-hunts. There was even a small book about holistic remedies. Many of the authors had a booth or service in the mall, and Natasha would send the eager readers over to get an autograph.

She had lain carpet on the floor a few months back to add color and class to her little slice of the flea market. It made the booth homier, and the basement floor wasn't so cold through her toes after standing on it for many hours. Long, velvet curtains covered the wooden slats that made up the walls of the booth. Most of the psychics used heavy velvet materials and posters to cover up the, ugly plain clapboard walls of the booths.

Natasha fiddled with, dusted and rearranged her stock until she grew bored. She even dusted some cobwebs off the large sign that had her name on it. *NATASHA: Medium to the Other Side.*

She took to her velvet chair with wooden claw feet, waiting for someone to come and sit in the matching one. She smiled at people who hurried by, looking at merchandise or gossiping about their tarot reading or crystal ball reading. She knew Gwen must

110

still be in town as she watched a few people wander past with Gwen's charts clutched tightly in their hands.

Gwen actually lived in Manhattan these days, but as a flight attendant, she was often landing in the Boston airport. When she had a few days off, she would stay in her favorite bed and breakfast in Hermana and hang out with her old friends. She always made the circle ceremonies. To her, they were more important than her job. She always said that without the circle, she would have nothing.

Gwen had studied astrology as a child; her mother was one of the most famous astrologers in the world. Gwen's mother had columns in newspapers and a client list that could fill a phone book. In keeping with tradition, Gwen had learned all about planets, transits and aspects. She could size up almost anyone just by knowing his or her birth date. Gwen's mother had taught her book knowledge combined with instinct. Neither one of them ever used a computer program to create forecasts, although for neatness's sake, Gwen created charts on a computer for her clients.

Natasha smiled as she thought about the circle and how the women were all going to consult Gwen's charts to create magic for love.

It seemed to be working for Maggie. Or was it?

Remembering Maggie kissing that guy that night still annoyed her. If Weldon had seen that, chances were that he would have broken up with her right then and there. Natasha had seen Maggie screw up good things before, so it would be no surprise to her if her relationship with Weldon crashed and burned before it even got started.

She grew weary of smiling at strangers and stood up again, fidgeting with a crystal ball. She didn't want to look into it; she was using all her energy to push away the spirits so she could have a clear head and peace for a moment.

The smudging and *feng shui* seemed to work at keeping the spirits at bay in her music room. She would have to have Ellie do her whole apartment—and soon. The lucky energy of her birthday only lasted a few days before and a few days after. Anything new she undertook during that time would last the year, or so the theory said. Even Gwen agreed with the idea of lucky birthday vibes.

Natasha dug through her purse to find the smudge stick she'd brought with her that day. The spirits were already peering out at her from the billows of her curtains, and she knew it wouldn't be long before they were jabbering in her ears again. She pulled out the stick and the small ceramic bowl of sand. As she lit the stick, the brush of spirits shifting around her, as if to see what she was doing, created a slight breeze. She held her hand over the blazing stick until it had burned down far enough to act like incense. She carefully blew out the flame over the bowl, sending bits of herb and sand scattering over her table.

She held the stick in one hand, the bowl in the other. Steady, dark smoke rolled up from the stick, and she walked around her booth, allowing it to waft up and down the curtains and into all the cracks where the spirits liked to hide.

The thick smell of the incense blended in with the rest of the flea market odors. Finally, she ground the stick out in the sand and put it aside. Satisfied that her booth was now more auspicious than ever, she returned to her comfy chair and watched more people stroll through the hallways.

Although she tried to look patient and inviting, she was aware that she was creepy-looking to strangers. Her long, dark hair and pale skin, coupled with her dark, penetrating eyes and dark clothes put people on edge. Now, she wore the giant locket with her long, black dress, and she imagined it was odd to the tourists as well. It was huge on her slender frame.

Fortune-tellers were easier to approach because their trades were obvious. A medium was more elusive, and she didn't have much business when she'd opened her booth. Although she was always willing to chat up new customers and gain some fresh appointments, the average person was spooked by ghosts and Ouija boards and of course, her gothic persona.

After a while, when it seemed as though no one would come to her booth, Natasha reached over to grab Madeline's latest book. It was an account of ghost-hunting around New England and opinions about which legends were true and which weren't. Madeline had an uncanny knack for capturing very intriguing sights and sounds. She had some orb pictures that couldn't be explained.

Natasha smiled. Of course orbs existed. She knew they existed, for she had been present when Madeline had taken pictures of them on multiple occasions.. If she could be a vampire with eternal life, why couldn't there be orbs? She could see dead people, so why couldn't some people see orbs? Why did it always have to be dust on the lens or some random reflection to explain the orb phenomenon?

Sometimes she found some people to be so very narrow-minded. Of course, they hadn't seen what she'd seen or done what she'd done.

There were many pictures of orbs in the book, and, as Natasha examined them, a shadow fell across the page. Looking up, she saw a worried man staring back at her. She had to restrain herself from leaping to her feet in joy.

"Gus?" she said, putting down the book.

"Yes. I didn't know if you would recognize me," he said softly. He was disheveled, as if he hadn't slept in days. His coat was torn, and his jeans were damp with snow and sand. A small, blue, knitted hat was pulled tightly over his short, blond hair.

"Why wouldn't I? I had a marvelous time New Year's Eve, didn't you?" Natasha asked. His eyes gleamed as she spoke, as if she were telling him he just won a million dollars.

"Of course I did." Gus waved his hands as if he had lots to say but couldn't find the words to say anything at all. "I was so happy to meet you."

"It was so sweet of you to remember my birthday too."

"Did you like the flowers?" Gus said. "You seemed like the type that could appreciate black roses."

"Most definitely. I just didn't know how to contact you to thank you."

"I'm here now."

"And thank you." Natasha smiled. They looked awkwardly at each other, Natasha sitting in her chair, staring up at him. Gus shifted his weight from foot to foot. Natasha noticed his work boots were soaked and leaving wet marks on her carpet. She'd have to remember to clean it up once he was gone. She indicated the chair across from her.

"Have a seat."

"Don't mind if I do," Gus said as he settled into the chair. His large, broad frame looked almost silly in the carved, wooden chair, as if he were a teddy bear in a dollhouse.

"So, what brings you to the flea market today?" Natasha asked, studying his chiseled cheeks and firm jaw line. As much as she liked Craig, she lamented that he didn't have the strong jaw Gus possessed.

"I wanted to see if you were here, and I wanted to buy a few things. So here I am."

"I'm here."

Gus looked around the booth from his chair and nodded. "You have some interesting things here. What is it exactly that you do?"

"I'm a medium," she said.

"No kidding. That's kind of cool. Like a ghost whisperer."

"It has its good points and its bad points."

Gus stared at her as if trying to see through her. He tilted his head as if to challenge her. "Do you really talk to ghosts? Isn't it all puppets and stuff?"

"I talk to ghosts. They're here," Natasha said as she waved her hand.

"There are ghosts here now?" Gus asked, looking up in the air.

"Of course there are ghosts here. We're in a flea market. All these antiques are swarming with souls trying to communicate."

"Creepy." Gus shuddered. He looked around as if

though expected to see one materialize right in front of him. Natasha was pleased to note the saging seemed to be keeping the pesky ones off to the edges of her booth.

"At first, yes, it's creepy. Very. Because you just don't know if you're crazy or if you're really seeing things. But then it's just annoying. Everywhere I go…" Natasha stopped and looked at Gus. "But enough about me. What do you do?"

"Me?" Gus laughed. "Me? My parents call me a bum, but really, I'm a writer."

Natasha nodded. "Ah yes, bum, writer…it's all the same. I know many writers."

"Are they bums?"

"None are rich, if that's what you mean."

"It's discouraging. I figure a place like Hermana would welcome the likes of me. An oddball with not a lot of bucks. Although lots of people around here seem to have very big bucks."

"There's a lot of old money in New England. Most of us have to work for a living, though. Like you. Like me," Natasha said. *A writer. That's worse than a musician.* "What kind of stuff do you write?"

"Stuff no one wants to read, that's for sure." Gus sighed, playing with his fingers. Natasha noticed how long and dark his eyelashes were. She wondered why it was that men always had the prettiest eyelashes.

"Are you published?" she asked.

"Not yet." Gus was sweating; his forehead was glowing under his little hat. A nervous, sweaty smell wafted from him and tickled Natasha's nose. She licked her lips, enjoying his masculine scent.

"Well, maybe one day you'll get published.

116

Maybe you'll let me read some of your stuff sometime."

"Sure. I'd like that. Hate to have it rot away in a drawer," Gus said.

"Well, will I like it?"

"Okay. Here's the thing. I've written a couple of very long stories, maybe they're books, I don't know, but they're all about love, and it's kind of embarrassing, really."

"You sound romantic," Natasha said, studying his torn pant leg. "Imagine that."

"Do you read romance?" Gus asked.

Natasha laughed. "Oh dear me, no. I can't st…well, let's just say I read a lot of action-adventure and some horror."

"Action-adventure? In books? I prefer mine in the movies. I want to see everything go down."

"Movies have their place. I love to go to the movies. Big screens, bigger sound."

"I like all the special effects in the big action scenes."

"Yes, I like them too."

They smiled at each other, and Natasha stood up. The hunger surged through her, roiling in her stomach.

"I didn't know if I'd see you again," Natasha said wistfully as she watched a couple walk by arm in arm. A pang of guilt shot through her. The feeling was familiar. The conversation was familiar. She imagined she had been in this kind of situation before. She'd have to read her diaries. Or maybe not.

There were many diaries she preferred not to read. There were boxes of them locked away in a storage locker. Hundreds of years of loves found and

117

lost. Memories made and broken. A heart that continued to beat despite the pain.

Once the memories were gone, it was for the better. Why relive pain and grief? Abandonment and loneliness? She preferred to read about her virgins' blood and spells.

Savanna had been right. Forgetting lovers was the best way to live even if she didn't learn from her mistakes.

If only she could forget Craig so fast.

"I was hoping I'd find you. I've been to your house a couple of times, but you never answer the door. I guess you're always working or playing your violin."

"Well, a girl has to practice. It's part of my livelihood. As well as...this." She waved her arm around.

"I hear you playing. You don't hear me ringing the bell. You need a louder doorbell."

"I'm so sorry, Gus. I'm not used to having visitors," Natasha said.

"Oh?" He stared at her, his eyes growing darker. "No visitors? Who do you practice with?" he asked. "I've heard more than one violin playing sometimes. Do you play with recorded music?"

Natasha went over to fiddle with Madeline's book. His questions stung at her as guilt flooded her. But why was she feeling guilty? She hadn't done anything wrong. She bet Maggie never felt guilty about anything.

"Sometimes, yes." Natasha turned to look at him while she held Madeline's book for comfort. "You're exactly right. I'll play along with recordings. It can really help sometimes."

118

"I see," Gus said as he stood up. "What do you have there?"

Natasha held it out to him. "My friend Madeline is a journalist and a ghost hunter. I guess these days she's more ghost hunter than journalist. At any rate, she's written a few books, and this is her latest."

Gus flipped through the pages. "Orbs. She's really into the orbs."

"Well, that book focuses a lot on the theories of orbs. She doesn't always write about orbs. Her books can be very factual."

"About ghosts? Factual stories about ghosts?" Gus teased.

"About the mysteries of haunted places. Of murder sites and suicides."

"And the crazy people who see ghosts." Gus smirked.

Natasha glared at him.

"I'm just teasing you, Natasha. Really I am. That's what we Gemini's do best."

Great, Natasha thought. *Another friggin' Gemini. Am I cursed or what?*" I know all about you Gemini's. Schizophrenics." Natasha leered.

"Touché. And you're correct." Gus grinned. "I'm a bona fide whack job. At your service." He took off his hat, his hair sticking crazily out in many directions as he deeply bowed to her. "In fact, Your Highness of Sanity and Ghosts, I came here to see if you want to go for lunch?"

"Right now?" Natasha didn't fancy the idea of going back out into the daylight, even if it was greatly overcast and snowing.

"Why not?" Gus offered her his arm as if they

were going to go skipping down the Yellow Brick Road.

"I'm not that spontaneous," Natasha said. "I just got here. I can't close down now."

Gus frowned. "What if I pretended I was your client? I'll pay you to do a séance for me," he said.

There was a ripple above Gus's head as he spoke. Natasha stared at it. There was someone trying to come through for him after all. Someone that could somehow rise above the saging. Someone or something strong. Or fresh.

The freshly dead had the strongest spirits, Natasha had learned over the years. They were more in-your-face and agitated, angrier at being dead than worrying about messages. But the older spirits were faded, weaker, and their agitations came from being muted, from communication breakdown.

The spirit above Gus shimmered briefly and faded.

"Okay," Natasha said. "We'll go. But how about we eat in the mall? There are a couple of okay restaurants here."

"Sounds fine. You pick," Gus said as Natasha closed down her booth.

They found a steakhouse where Natasha enjoyed a rare steak and a glass of red wine. She ate quickly as the blood dripped from her meat and onto the plate. The pungent aroma of Gus made her light-headed. There was a musky, dangerous smell to him, something animal-like. A hunting smell. She pushed aside her baked potato and announced herself full.

"You really liked your steak," Gus said.

Natasha smiled; the bloody, salty taste was still in

her mouth. It quelled the hunger for a moment. "I do. I love steak. The rarer, the better. I see you do too."

Gus had also finished his rare steak as well as his loaded baked potato and broccoli florets. He leaned back, content as he sipped his red wine. He rubbed his swollen stomach. "That was quite a feast. Yet oddly enough, I'm still hungry," he said quite seriously.

"I am too," Natasha said. Her stomach rumbled in agreement.

Gus heard it and stared. "What sort of things do you hunger for?" He asked with a twinkle in his eye.

"Chocolate," Natasha said. "Isn't that what all normal girls crave?"

Gus raised an eyebrow. "And you crave chocolate, like a normal girl?"

"Yes, I do."

"Although there's nothing normal about you," Gus said, taking Natasha's hand from across the table.

"I hope you mean that in a good way," she said.

"You are beautiful as well as mysterious. I like that."

"Thank you."

Gus paid the bill, and they went over to a bakery kiosk and bought pieces of chocolate mousse cake. As they sat in the food court, Natasha happened to glance up at one of the televisions. A picture of Pete was on the newscast.

"Oh my." Natasha sighed. "Poor Pete."

Gus looked up at the monitor. "That guy. Poor chap. Mauled by a bear."

"Is that what happened?"

"Must be. What else could do that?"

Natasha shuddered. "To think, it could have been me."

121

"Why you?" Gus asked. His dark eyes were large with interest. Natasha thought she could see herself in them for a moment. They weren't romantic and kind like Craig's. They were moody and intense. Dark thoughts and darker secrets. Her heart raced faster, and a thrill surged through her heart.

"I was out that night too. Not far from where he was attacked." She shuddered again. "Imagine."

Gus shook his head as he popped a spoonful of mousse into his mouth. He savored it for a moment. "You'll never come to harm. I'll make sure of that." He wiped his lips with his napkin.

"Ah yes, my knight in shining armor. They said he would arrive," Natasha mocked, waving her hand like a queen.

"Who? Those witches?" Gus pointed in the direction of Lucy's house.

"My friends, you mean," Natasha said haughtily.

"Yes, your friends. The witches. This town's full of them, that's for sure."

"Can't have a witch town without them," Natasha said.

Gus nodded. Natasha snickered and ate her mousse. "So they think I'm your knight?" he asked.

"Not really." His face fell as she spoke. "I mean, I don't mean 'not really,' I just mean that it's not specific. This stuff."

"Well, maybe one day I will be your knight in shining armor," he said as he stood up. "But first, we still have to do one more thing."

"What's that?" Natasha asked.

"A séance, of course," Gus said, his face animated once more.

He took Natasha back to her booth to properly lock up and retrieve her coat. She was glad it was late afternoon and it would be dark out already. Or at least gray enough to shield her delicate skin from the sun. There was no use in going through the ordeal of getting virgin blood if one was just going to wander around in the sunlight anyway. Mortals were lucky that the living cells in their bodies protected them slightly better from the sun's harmful rays. Still, Natasha had seen many a sun worshipper in her day age before her time.

She didn't wonder if Lucy had lain around in the sun in her youth as well. But then again, she had no clue as to Lucy's real age, although general gossip put her in her eighties. The family was so well documented that Natasha knew she could figure it out if she had to.

So, if Lucy was in her eighties, Natasha didn't want to think about how old she was. And yet here she was, aroused by the broad shoulders and dark, mysterious eyes of Gus.

"We'll go here," Gus proclaimed as they stood in front of one of the hotels near the mall. The Village Knoll was old and still standing on its original foundation. In fact, much of the mall had been built around it, because it couldn't be demolished since it was a historical monument. Great men had stayed there over the years. Presidents, shipping merchants and religious leaders had all rested their heads in the Village Knoll's pine rooms.

Gus took her by the hand and led her into the ostentatious lobby. A giant crystal chandelier hung from the ceiling, and there were two sets of staircases leading to the second level on either side of the front doors. The runners had a pattern of green and gold diamonds while the main carpet was a deep forest green. Between the chandeliers, the garish carpeting and the stained-glass windows, Natasha was getting a headache. So much refraction and light.

She was ready to follow him up the stairs, when he stopped and stared around the lobby. "Okay," he muttered to himself.

Natasha was even more surprised when he sat down in one of the lobby's overstuffed chairs by some potted plants. She noted the plants quivered as she approached the chair next to his.

"This is the perfect place," he said proudly.

"The lobby of a hotel?" she asked, narrowing her eyes.

"Why not?"

Natasha held her tongue and sat down. The plants near to her yellowed and curled, their leaves trying to escape as they shriveled up. Natasha pretended not to notice the plants' sudden demise and hoped that Gus wouldn't, either.

Natasha took a deep breath and looked around. The lobby was opulent, but too many spirits were here. As they caught wind of the medium in the room, they flittered in from all around, like curious children discovering Santa was in the building. She saw the ripple above Gus's head shimmer, and she knew it wouldn't be long before whoever it was would reveal him or herself.

"I suppose it's as good of a place as any," she said.

The lobby was busy as people bustled back and forth. Bellhops hauled suitcases up the winding staircases, and maids ran around with piles of fresh,

124

white linens. Tourists wandered in, disoriented and dazed, dragging their wheeled suitcases behind them.

Natasha thought that for January, the hotel was doing very well indeed. It felt more like a train station than a place to sleep.

Gus took out a handkerchief and wiped his forehead. His hair was still messy from his hat, and his face glowed.

"It's getting hot in here," he said, dark eyes peering at everyone who walked by them.

"Is it? I find it a bit drafty myself." Natasha pulled her coat around herself tighter.

"See? It's so damn hot they're killing the plants," Gus said as he pointed to the withered plant beside Natasha.

"I thought plants liked heat."

"Well, that one isn't too happy," Gus said as he pulled his sweater over his head. There were large sweat stains under his arms and across his back. Natasha smelled him, strong and nervous. Was she making him anxious?

He unbuttoned the first few buttons on his shirt, and Natasha remembered the precious moments they'd had alone at Lucy's house before they'd been interrupted. As she stared at him, she knew she wanted to feel his hands on her body, his lips on hers, him inside of her, caressing her from the inside out.

Gus watched the people who kept coming and going through the heavy glass doors. "Are we too close to the main doors? Is that going to mess with your karma?"

Natasha glared at him and shook her head.

"Sorry," he said. "I don't know when to shut up

sometimes." His legs jiggled nervously, and he cracked his knuckles.

Natasha looked over at the lobby staircase. More restless spirits were on parade. She thought she would lose her mind. Where were they all coming from? They couldn't possibly all be from this hotel.

It didn't matter. Ghosts came and went, and just that idea was enough to make some people go mad.

Natasha just accepted what she saw, as she always did, and turned to Gus. He was very pale, and sweat beaded his forehead.

"What's wrong with you? It's not that hot," she said.

Gus shook his head. "No. It's me. I've been fighting a fever. I think it's come back." He dabbed his forehead again. "I must need more cowbell," he weakly joked.

"Yeah, right." Natasha laughed halfheartedly. The man was going to make her nuts. Or maybe it was the ghosts. Or maybe it was the dead plant that was now nothing but crumbled dust in the pot. She noted some of the farther-away plants were growing brown and withered.

Gus leaned forward, putting his face into his hands. He was flushed, and his five-o'clock shadow was more pronounced. Natasha noted how large and strong his fingers were; his knuckles were huge. She imagined those hands touching her in her most secret spots.

As Gus curled into himself, Natasha studied his broad shoulders. His shirt, though unbuttoned, seemed too tight on him, the seams straining as if they would burst open at any moment.

"Oh, I don't know if I can even do this séance now," Gus said through his fingers. "I can't believe how bad I feel. Maybe I should just go home."

"Are you going to be sick? Do you have food poisoning?" Natasha stood up and went over to him, cradling his head against her. He tried to push her away.

"I'm so hot."

"I'll drive you. Where do you live?" Natasha said, trying to nudge his face up.

"No, it's okay. I don't need a ride. It's too far. Really." Gus stood up, his legs wobbling a bit as he tried to put his sweater back on. It didn't fit at all; his hands barely made it through the armholes. In frustration, he threw the sweater back on the chair and grabbed his coat.

Gus shook his head sadly as he turned to face Natasha. His face was shadowy, flushed with sweat, though oddly changed. She couldn't quite put her finger on what was different about him, but something definitely was. His eyes seemed more sunken in.

"I'm sorry we didn't get to the séance. But here's money for your trouble." Gus pulled a wad of bills from his pocket and peeled off a few. He swayed back and forth as if he were trying to keep balance on a ship. He shakily held the money out to Natasha.

She pushed his hand away. "Oh please, you don't have to do that. I don't have a pimp to answer to."

"Then let me take you out again." Gus coughed several times and then wiped his whole face with the handkerchief.

"It's a date. We'll do this again. But really, I don't mind taking you somewhere. Maybe you're having an allergic reaction to food or something."

"I'm okay. Really."

Before Natasha could say anything else, Gus hurried off through the lobby, pushing by people as he staggered toward the entrance. As he approached the doors, he grabbed one of the maids and pointed at the dead plant beside Natasha.

The maid looked over to where he was pointing and nodded as he pushed his way out to the street.

Natasha watched him stumble down the sidewalk. Then he was gone.

She stared blankly after him.

What on earth was that all about?

Just as puzzling, when she looked back toward the stairs, all the hovering spirits had disappeared. Every last one of them. It was as if the show was over and they had all gone home.

She turned back to where Gus had been sitting. His imprint in the chair was still there. The essence of his presence hadn't quite faded. His thick-sweat smell still permeated her nostrils.

The maid who had been talking to Gus approached Natasha's area but then stopped as she stared around the lobby. All the plants had transformed from green to brown. The ones nearest to Natasha were fragments of dust. The maid touched the brittle branches of one of the tall palm trees near the door. The tree fell over, dust spraying across the carpet.

"*Sacré bleu!*" the maid cursed. "Get a broom," she yelled to the porter. "And a vacuum cleaner. There's a mess over here."

As the porter radioed for a broom, and the maid looked up at all of the hanging plants. They were limp and brown as well.

128

"This town…no one can keep plants alive in this town…there's always something, someone. Just got them all looking good, then bam," the maid muttered as she examined the pots. She fussed and fiddled, making her way over to Natasha, where the devastation was the worst.

"What has happened here? These were just watered." The maid wasn't talking to anyone in particular, nor was she expecting any explanations. Natasha watched her peer into the pots, touching the dead plants and poking at the earth in great puzzlement.

Natasha wondered if she should order a few trees and have them sent over anonymously. After all, it was her fault the plants were now dead. Of course, that would be fine until Gus wanted to return to the lobby the next time he wanted a séance, and then the plant killing would begin again. The idea amused her for a moment until her thoughts returned to ponder Gus's weirdness.

Poor guy was sick. But he wasn't *sick* sick. She knew that because she could smell sickness. A cold, the flu, cancer and AIDS all had a certain kind of aroma about them. An illness that was terminal smelled different than a passing bug. Mental illness smelled different then sadness. Food poisoning was easy to spot, as was a tension headache or pregnancy nausea.

Whatever Gus's problem was, it had nothing to do with a cold or food poisoning. Something dark was inside him, and it was trying to come out. Or maybe it had come out. The sweat pouring from him, the strange way his face looked as he left and even the way his clothes didn't seem to fit right all pointed to something.

Maybe that was why he wanted the séance.

She stared at where he had sat, pushing all thoughts out of her mind, hoping to "see" what it was she needed to "see."

The shimmering that had been above Gus at the flea market coasted over his chair. It flared out for a moment to reveal a face and then poofed away just as suddenly.

"Pete?" she asked.

The spirit was gone.

Chapter Eleven

Someone will ask a favor of you.

Natasha and Maggie Talk

Natasha wanted to sage her music room that night but remembered she had left her sage stick at the booth. She knew if she didn't keep up a regular routine of saging, the ghosts would return to the room and make her nuts.

The crowds in the mall were thinning out, and the flea market was even quieter. Very few booths were still open when she returned. People turned their heads as she hurried down the aisles, her boots thumping as she walked. Her agitation was contagious.

What was up with Gus? Maybe he had felt all those spirits too and couldn't take it. Some people got very ill when they encountered ghosts or other electromagnetic situations.

She found her sage stick, finished the rest of her cleaning tasks, and was just putting the padlock on the latch when she noticed someone watching her. He was a thin, wiry man with a large, bald head. His shoulder and right arm twitched as he stared at her.

"Hello," she said. "Can I help you?" *Why is everyone so neurotic today?* she wondered. *Now this one is a bundle of nerves as well.*

"I'm not too late, am I?" he asked. "I wanted a reading."

He stood in front of her, trying to pull himself taller, his feet dancing back and forth. But Natasha still towered over him.

"Oh, I don't do readings. I do séances, and I usually don't do them here, either." Natasha instinctively reached for her amulet under her coat. It was very hot.

"How do I do it, then? Make an appointment?" the man asked. He seemed nervous, but most people asking for a séance were rather nervous the first time and worse at the séance.

"You can make an appointment," Natasha said.

"You have a place?" he asked.

"No. I'll come to you."

His face twitched into a smile. He stared at her almost as if he recognized her from somewhere. Of course, he could have seen her almost anywhere. At psychic fairs, at concerts, at clubs. She was all over the place.

"You'll come to me. That's great. Fantastic." He took the card she held out to him. It trembled in his fingers as he nervously pulled his wallet out from his trousers. He opened the wallet and fumbled as he slid the card in. He shoved the wallet back into his pants.

"Now it's safe," he said proudly.

"Give me a call," she instructed. "What's your name?"

"Bob."

"Okay, Bob. When you call, I'll remember you."

Bob nodded excitedly. "Thank you, ma'am.

132

Thank you." She watched as he walked away. A chill crawled up her back.

That wasn't his real name.

Of course, lots of people who went to psychics used a fake name, as if they were doing something *wrong* and might get caught.

The name was one thing, but there was something even odder about his aura.

As she finished locking up, she tried to put her finger on what it was that disturbed her about Bob. She closed her eyes again and tried to see what she had just seen around him.

Rings of blackness.

But that wasn't so unusual in depressed people. Especially right after Christmas in freezing-cold New England. The swells of blackness hadn't troubled her. There was more.

A haze.

A sense that she wasn't seeing his true face.

"Penny for your thoughts?" Maggie's voice startled her.

"Oh, you're still here," Natasha exclaimed. "I had no idea."

"Yep, just closing up." She nodded. "My last client was odd," she added. "Actually, my last two were odd. One was that weird guy that just left you. And the other was some dude named Jim Hawthorne who was at a séance you did."

"Oh." Just the name of Jim Hawthorne sent a chill up her back. "What did he want?"

"I'm not sure. He made me do a couple of throws about you, but I wasn't sure what he was asking or if I was even giving him the right information."

133

"Like what did he ask?"

"He's one of those people who just say a name and think you already know what they want to know. You know, because we have nothing else on our minds but that person and all the millions of issues and problems rattling around in their heads. Anyway, when I get those kinds of people, I just look at the cards and try to intuit. But on him, it was really tough."

"I remember him. There was something about him I didn't like. He creeped me out," Natasha said.

"Well, he seemed to like you. That's why I couldn't tell if he was trying to find out more about you to ask you out, or what. "

"You'd think he'd just ask."

"Sometimes they get embarrassed when they know you know people they know. If you know what I mean," Maggie said with a nod. "Whew."

Natasha and Maggie walked down the hallway

"What about that weirdo? That little, bald guy. He told me his name was Bob. He came to you too?" Natasha said.

"He told me his name was Tim." Maggie shivered as she thought back to him. "He was plenty weird. I don't know at all what he was getting at. But he seemed pretty happy with the reading I gave him."

"Was he trying to talk to the dead?"

"No. Well, he did ask one question about his father, who had recently died."

"What did he ask?"

"I can't really tell you the details. You know. Ethics and all. I can tell you the response was more of a character study."

"Maybe he just misses him. He wants me to contact someone. Maybe it's dear old Dad."

"Perhaps." Maggie nodded. "Hey, want to go for a drink?"

"Sure."

Once they settled in at a table at Intuition and ordered drinks, Maggie turned to Natasha.

"Do you mind if I call Weldon and tell him I'm going to be a bit late? We're supposed to meet for drinks."

"So go to him," Natasha said. "Why the hell are you sitting here with me?"

"I want to know about Gus! I saw him at your booth," Maggie said as she pulled out her cell phone. She text-messaged a note to Weldon.

"Oh...you did..." Natasha said, already almost forgetting he'd been there at all. "Yes, he did stop by for a bit."

"Yes, I'm so curious I could burst," Maggie said as she pressed Send.

"You know curiosity killed the cat," Natasha said with a deadpan expression.

"But I want to know what happened." Maggie leaned forward, grabbing Natasha's arm. "Did he ask you out or what?"

"Why do you want to know so badly?"

"Because it's so romantic!" Maggie's phoned buzzed, and she checked the message from Weldon.

Natasha thought back to her last image of Gus's massive form running from the hotel. The darkness of his emotions, the dying plants crumbling in the lobby. The haunted face of Pete and the other ghosts. It didn't feel at all romantic to her. "Well, he came by to say hi, that's all."

"And? Jeez, Natasha, you have to stop being so

coy." Maggie pushed Natasha's arm. "So, what happened? You guys gonna get jiggy, or what? Do you still like him? Huh?"

"I think we're going to see each other again. He kind of wasn't feeling well and left."

"Oh. That sucks. Hope it was nothing you said," Maggie joked.

Natasha sipped her wine. "You know, Maggie, I'm not very good with men. Sure, I'm great with the advice and all for others, but personally, I'm just not good with men."

"Natasha, I'm sure you're fine."

"No. I'm not good at all. You see, I went for so long with no men. Just being single. Hanging with my girls. Doing my work, the circle. I feel pretty complete without a man in my life."

"And now Gus has come in!" Maggie squealed. "You're so lucky."

Natasha put down her wineglass and stared sternly at Maggie. "It's not that. It's not that at all. There's Craig."

Maggie's mouth hung open for a moment. "Get out!" she said in her best Elaine-from-*Seinfeld* impression.

"Yes, I like two guys." Natasha hung her head. "I'm so confused. I don't know what to do. I went from nothing to too much."

"Oh." Maggie nodded. "I see where this is going."

"No, you don't. You have no idea what's going on. Now listen, here's the thing. I met Gus New Year's Eve. We fooled around a little but not a lot, you know? Then I had to hurry off, and we never traded numbers.

136

He must have asked around about me because he knows where I live."

"It's not like no one knows who you are in Hermana," Maggie said.

"I know that. But still, he took the effort to find me. He left me a bouquet of black roses on my birthday. He said he's been by but I never answer the door."

"Well, it's true. You don't. I've dropped by myself and can't get you to open up that door until you're done practicing or sleeping or whatever the hell it is you do all day long."

Natasha nodded. "But, Maggie, I'm in a quandary. I've been jamming with Craig, and I really like him. He doesn't have the animal magnetism Gus has, but we enjoy music. He's a fantastic guitar player, and he doesn't have such a huge ego that he's impossible to jam with. Our music is so beautiful, a lovely give-and-take kind of thing."

"So keep playing with Craig."

"But now I'm sleeping with Craig."

"No! Are you sleeping with Gus too?"

"I told you, I've barely even seen the guy at all. We made out New Year's Eve, and since then there's been nothing."

"How's Craig in bed?"

"He's fantastic. God, it's like we're meant to be together. He plays me like he plays his guitar. It's just that..."

"What?"

"Well, he's a small, little man, and I like my guys big and strong, like Gus."

"Then go for Gus."

137

"But Craig is so attentive. I can't jam with Gus."

"Then go for Craig."

"But I...I don't know if I can be with Craig for long. I don't know."

"Well...what's wrong with two guys?"

"I'm not a two-guy kind of girl, Maggie. Hell, I'm not even a one-guy kind of girl, I don't think."

"Nonsense. You can juggle a couple of men for a little while 'til you get to know them both a bit more."

"It's so stressful already and it's just started."

"Well, let's think about this. What signs are they?"

Natasha laughed. "You're never going to believe it. They're *both* Gemini's. How crazy is that? I can't even pick one of them based on a sign!"

Maggie laughed and shook her head.

"Wow, you have your hands full. Well, why don't you take your own advice? Open heart and open mind and see where it takes you."

Natasha sighed. "Yes, open mind, open heart. I guess I'll just see what happens next."

Chapter Twelve

You may have some difficult decisions to make today.

Natasha Makes a Choice

Natasha woke to the wind howling outside her windows. Another snowy day in Hermana. She didn't want to get out of bed. The chill in the room made her pull the covers up, and she debated whether she would go out at all. But then she remembered she was supposed to go see Craig's band play that night with Maggie and Ellie.

She dragged herself up and over to the shower. She ignored the ghostly chatter around her as she lathered up with her scented soaps.

Craig.

Gus.

It was so weird to be attracted to two men at the same time.

She washed her hair and applied conditioner to it twice in the hope of drowning out any of her natural smells with the flowery aromas.

Once she was finished in the shower, she dried

herself off and powdered her body from head to toe with floral-scented talcum.

She applied makeup to her face, staring at her dark eyes in the mirror. The wrinkles were starting to show again. Not only did she have her constant hunger to worry about, but she had to do something about her looks too. When her looks started to fade, she was pretty sure she didn't smell so hot either.

She spritzed a large dose of perfume over her naked body and into her hair.

Another birthday come and gone. At least on this one, she was lucky enough to have a full moon and a circle. How often would a girl be lucky enough to have that happen?

The women were happy to use her birthday as an opportunity to redefine themselves and their love goals. She wondered if and how the new theory of combining Gwen's charts and Ellie's *feng shui* with a birthday would activate romantic love.

She had to make sure she had Ellie over sometime to *feng shui* the rest of her home. Once her makeup was set and her clothes fastened and buckled, she went over to her computer. She checked her horoscope and saw that "changes were in the air." The horoscope both amused and annoyed her.

Wasn't there always some kind of change in the air?

She read through her emails, mostly junk, but as she was about to close them, one caught her eye.

She pulled it up and saw it was from Gus.

Hello, Natasha.
I'm sorry I had to run off the other day. I got your

email from your business card at the booth. I hope you
don't mind. I would really like to see you again
sometime. I promise I won't run away.
    Gus

Natasha smiled, reading and rereading the email
as if she could find a hidden message snuggled among
the words.

She imagined that him finding her email and
taking the time to write was indication enough that he
was still interested. She wondered why he didn't
phone her, but she imagined that maybe he was
embarrassed about his sudden exit and he didn't want
to put her on the spot if he should call and she wanted
nothing to do with him.

She typed and retyped, trying to find the words to
send him. She wrote a rather long email but decided to
erase it. She didn't even know the guy, so why was she
pouring out her heart and soul?

In the end, she eagerly wrote a succinct response.

Dear Gus
    I would love to see you again. Name a date and
let's see what we can do.
    Natasha

She sent the email and waited to see if it went
through. Once she was satisfied it was merrily on its
way, she shut down her computer.

A surge of happiness swelled through her.
Whatever Gus's problem had been, it had nothing to
do with her. She had suspected that was the case, but
now she knew.

A scratching sound outside her window startled her. She ran over to see what it was. When she looked out, all she could see was thick clumps of snow coming down. The sound had likely been the snow hitting the windowpane.

No matter. Between the ghosts, the weather and the energy of the town itself, something new and strange was always going on.

She hurried around the apartment, gathering up her purse and coat. With a sigh, she went out to greet the night.

Intuition was crowded, but Maggie and Ellie had found a table near the stage. Natasha was covered in snow when she sat down.

"Look, it's the Abominable Natasha," Maggie joked.

"Ha-ha. Very funny," Natasha said as she pulled off her coat.

"Your guy is looking at you." Ellie grinned. Natasha looked over at the stage, and Craig beamed at her as he strummed his guitar.

"It's so fun to have a musician boyfriend," Maggie said. "You can imagine that every song he plays is just for you."

"He's not my boyfriend," Natasha said. "We jammed together a couple of times."

"Was it fun?" Ellie asked.

"It was lots of fun. But, quite frankly, I think I'm more attracted to Gus. "

"Really?" Maggie asked. "But you don't even know where he lives. Or what he does."

"I know he's a writer. He lives in Hermana somewhere. He sent me an email today."

Maggie sat forward excitedly. "What did it say?"

"It was just a simple request for a date," Natasha said.

"And what did you say?" Ellie pressed.

"I accepted, of course. I just don't know when."

"Maybe he's emailing you right now," Ellie said.

"Maybe, but I'm here with you guys. I'm not sitting around the house waiting for some guy."

The set was over, and Craig came over to the table. He kissed Natasha on the cheek.

"How's it going, Natasha?" he asked.

"I'm doing great, thanks," she replied. "And you?"

"I'm happy to see you."

Natasha nodded. Maggie nudged Ellie.

"Let's go out for a smoke," Maggie said to Ellie.

"Sure thing."

Maggie winked at Natasha as the ladies left. Craig scooted his chair closer.

"So, when do you want to get together again to jam?" he asked. "I do enjoy our sessions."

Natasha took a deep breath. She even surprised herself when she spoke. "I'm sorry, Craig. But I'm going to have to stop seeing you."

Craig frowned. "But why? Did I do something wrong?"

"Not at all," Natasha said as she petted his hand. "You're a great guy. A wonderful guy. And a fantastic musician. But I'm going to have to stop seeing you."

"There's someone else?" he asked.

"I don't know," Natasha said. "I'm kind of confused, and I don't want to hurt you."

Craig's eyes were sad. "Is there anything I can do to change your mind?"

"I need to think. And I don't want you waiting around for me."

Craig sighed heavily and drank his beer. "It's because you think I'm a flaky musician who can't be stable, isn't it?"

"No, it's not. Believe me, this town is full of flakes."

"So why can't we hang out?"

"We just can't. I'm sorry."

Craig stared at her. He fidgeted for a moment and then stood up.

"All right, Natasha. I'll respect your decision. But if you change your mind, even about jamming, *just jamming*, please let me know. We make beautiful music together." He tried to smile, but it seemed false. He left her to return to his bandmates.

When Ellie and Maggie arrived, they were all smiles. "So?" Maggie asked.

"I broke up with him," Natasha said.

"What?" Ellie asked. "You were just talking about how much you like him."

Natasha looked sadly toward the stage. "I do like him. But I like Gus too. I can't juggle two guys."

"But he's the real deal. He likes you a lot. You can see it in his eyes. And he's here, and Gus isn't," Maggie said.

"I know. I can't explain it. There's just something about Gus that I need to explore. Maybe I won't like him after all and I'll regret hurting Craig. I don't know," Natasha said fretfully. "I have to get out of here."

"Do you want us to come with you?" Maggie asked.

"No, I think I just want to be alone for now."

Natasha put on her coat and glanced once more at Craig. He was busy tuning his guitar for the next set. She would miss his wiry, little body and his *joie de vivre*. But she was drawn to Gus's darkness.

The snow had stopped falling, and Natasha wandered through the cobblestone streets, wondering if she had acted too quickly in cutting Craig loose. However, the more she walked, the more she was sure she had made the right decision.

She was hungry and hated it.

Why couldn't her meals hold her appetite at bay longer?

Part of the reason she had broken up with Craig was that she didn't know if she could stop herself with him. His blood made her mad with desire.

Each time they made love, she was closer to wanting to consume him. To drink of that lively musician blood and feel it coursing through her veins. She had already gone farther than she should have with him. Luckily at this point, he just thought she had a weird fetish, but if she one day went too far, he would be one more person to know her secret. She didn't want to hurt him or kill him. He had too much to offer the world.

On the other hand, if he got to know her too well, he would wonder about her strange habits. How she stayed young. How she slept all day and wandered the streets all night.

In the distance, she heard a wolf howling. The sound was mournful and soared through her body.. She ached as the wolf howled again. A howl and a little yelp. A cry. Like grief. Like the world was a dark, hollow void of emptiness. She felt like the wolf sounded. Alone and sad.

After a few minutes, there was another strange sound in the air. A low, humming noise tickled her senses. She wasn't sure if she was hearing it or feeling it. It was almost like the steady vibration of a motorboat approaching the docks, but the sound wasn't coming from the water. Besides, who would be foolish enough to take a boat out in a January snowstorm?

She stopped walking and grew more curious about the humming sound. She hadn't recalled hearing it before last month. She had been walking the streets, the beach and the forests of Hermana for decades. She was familiar with most of the noises of the night. This noise was new, and it piqued her curiosity.

However, it was becoming apparent that the sound was happening more frequently on her late night sojourns through the town.

She was determined to figure out where it was coming from. She closed her eyes, turned around and walked until she determined the source must be in the woods. Maybe it was some kind of generator. Maybe there was a new home in the woods or some kind of work being done. It was far too cold and blowy to go traipsing through the woods that night, but she was determined to get to the bottom of it soon.

It was likely no big mystery, but so little amused her these days.

Her bones ached from the cold, and her face felt like a wooden slat of splinters. Between the grueling weather and her decaying body, she wanted to lie down on the beach and have the icy, cold fingers of the ocean pull her out to sea.

Instead, she needed to do what she could to right herself in her own little world. Her aches and pains could and would be dealt with, even though she never truly enjoyed what she had become.

She continued until she passed by a warehouse where there was loud music. Dozens of teenagers and young people spilled out into the streets, smoking cigarettes and laughing. She decided to see what was going on. By the brightly colored clothes of the partiers, she knew it was a rave.

Young people went to raves.

She needed to be around young people.

Her senses tingled and twitched as the youthful energy slammed into her, taking hold in her body. An urgency surged through her and she knew she was in the right place. The scent was here, and she would follow it until she found what she needed.

She paid the $10 cover charge and went inside. Kids jumping around to techno music packed the dance floor. Their glowing, sweaty bodies were bumping and grinding. Fashion was a garish combination of fluorescent greens and oranges in polka dots and plaids. The black lights on the dance floor added a heightened unreality to pallor of the skin, and eyes glowed weirdly, as if she had wandered onto another planet. She noted with interest that most of the dancers were girls in skimpy clothes. Many of the girls wore ponytails or short, spiked hair. The boys had both long and short hair, with a few multicolored Mohawks towering above the rest.

The smells of sweat and sexual fever invaded her nostrils. She stared at the dance floor, but what she sought wasn't there. She followed her nagging senses down one of the hallways and into the basement level. There was another dance floor where jungle tribal music boomed through her feet.

The kids were dancing in a sweaty throng to the music but she wasn't going to enter the room.

She continued on.

The sensation grew stronger, and soon her fingers and breasts burned. She was close, so close.

Around the corner was the bathroom, and she went inside. She took off her coat and hung it on the hook. As she sat in the stall, she could hear some girls giggling outside the door.

"He's so cute. I could just die," one girl said.

"So go for it," her friend said.

"I can't. He doesn't go for virgins."

"You don't know that."

"Yes, I do. He wants girls that put out. It's too bad."

The girls gossiped and giggled as they put on their makeup. When Natasha came out, she stood beside them, brushing her hair. The girls wore miniskirts and tank tops, applying rich, red lipstick to their young, pouty lips. Natasha glanced over at them. The blonde smiled at her.

"I like your hair," the girl said. "And your necklace."

"Thank you."

"Tell her she shouldn't be so shy around guys," her redheaded friend said.

"What's the problem?" Natasha asked.

The blonde rolled her eyes. "I like this guy but I don't think he likes me."

"Why not?"

"Because I don't put out," the girl sulked.

"So, pick another guy, then," Natasha said.

"But I like this guy. He's cute and funny. He's so hot."

"Well, talk to him," Natasha offered.

"I do talk to him. We're in the same college classes."

"Then he knows you exist."

"Yeah...but..."

"Don't worry. If it's meant to be, it's meant to be," Natasha said, applying more eye shadow.

"God, you sound like my mother," the blonde said.

Natasha cringed. "I'm sorry. I don't know what else to say."

"I bet you have a guy," the blonde said. "You're so pretty."

"Why thank you, but actually, I have no one right now," Natasha said. "I'm single and have been for a very long time."

"Why?"

"Why, indeed? Well, let's just say I like having my freedom. Men can really mess that up for us, you know? You get with a guy and next thing you know, you're cooking, cleaning and doing their laundry. Then you have kids. And then you've lost who ever you were. Just enjoy life."

The girls stared at Natasha.

"I've heard that before too," the blonde said.

"Well, would you feel better if I bought you a drink?" Natasha asked.

The blonde nodded. "Sure."

The three women went over to the bar, and Natasha bought a round of orgasms.

149

"Here's to woman power," Natasha said as she clinked her glass against theirs. The girls giggled as they downed their drinks.

"That's so good," the blonde said. "Thank you."

"Oh, they're playing my song," the redhead said. "Let's go dance."

"You go on. I'm going to stay here," Natasha said as she looked at the writhing bodies on the dance floor. "The beat is a bit fast for me."

"I'm going to stay here," the blonde said.

The redhead danced away, and the blonde turned to Natasha.

"Do you smoke?" she asked.

"Yes."

"I don't mean tobacco," the young woman said. "Want to go outside?"

"All right." Natasha's heart beat quickly as she was led outside. The youthful steps as the stranger looked for a dark alley away from the club made Natasha giddy. This girl was so lively, so innocent, a virgin.

In the distance, above the thrum of the music and the chatter of the people, Natasha still heard, or rather felt the humming vibration she had sensed earlier. She cocked her head, trying to figure out if it was still coming from the woods, but it was too hard to tell with all the noise around her.

At last, the girl was satisfied with a spot that was secluded. She opened her purse and pulled out a joint.

"What's your name, anyway?" the girl asked.

"Natasha."

"I'm Sandy. Pleased to meet you." The girl shivered as she tried to light the joint. The wind had picked up, and it was snowing again.

"You know, I don't live too far from here," Natasha said. "Do you want to go do that at my place and then come back? We won't be long."

Sandy looked at Natasha, the unlit joint in her hand. "Really?"

"Sure, why not?"

Natasha led the girl up her back staircase and into the music room. "Get comfortable while I get us some drinks," she said.

"Sure thing," Sandy said, walking around the room looking at the instruments. "This place is really cool."

Natasha went through the door and into her apartment. The ghosts pressed down on her, and she shrugged them away as she opened her cupboards. A small vial of clear liquid was way in the back of the top shelf. She poured a few drops into a glass, then added some red wine. The other glass held only red wine.

When she returned, Sandy was sitting on the couch.

How familiar it all felt. How sad she was to lure this innocent girl here like this. But it was all about survival of the fittest.

Sandy drank the wine and smoked the joint, babbling on as the marijuana coursed through her system. Natasha let her prattle, knowing that soon, she would be silenced forever.

When the girl finally fell asleep, Natasha left her on the couch. She put her coat back on and returned to the club.

"Hey, have you seen Sandy?"The redhead came up to Natasha as the lights flicked on and the revelers started pouring out of the club.

"No, I haven't. Did she finally meet up with that guy?"

"I don't know. I haven't seen her all night."

"Strange. Well, if I see her, I'll tell her that you were looking for her."

Satisfied that her alibi was set, Natasha left the club and returned home to complete her grisly task.

Chapter Thirteen

Get your affairs in order. Clean your clutter and organize your mind.

Natasha Tries Again

Natasha checked her email and seeing no response from Gus, despaired that maybe she had done the wrong thing in breaking up with Craig.

What was wrong with her, anyway?

She and Craig were so perfectly suited. They made great music together, and he was fabulous in bed. He never asked her for anything, so why did she throw him away so hastily?

She was crazy, that was all.

She touched her cheek lightly and smiled as the fresh skin was smooth under her fingers. Sandy really had been a virgin, and Natasha was good for another year or two.

Natasha recalled that not that long ago, a virgin lasted for at least ten years. But as gravity took its toll, or as Lucy said, the body crumbled, the spell length was getting shorter.

Back in the '70's—and possibly even before then;

she couldn't remember anymore—she had tried to avoid the kill. It was so horrible, to kill innocent girls who were trying so hard to be respectful and productive people. Or at least, respectful in that they were saving their virtue for that one special guy.

The guys never would have appreciated them anyway. Sure, they would have gotten their virginity, but once the novelty was gone, most men would be back out on the streets tomcatting around with any old women. She wanted to scream to some of the girls that they might as well fuck as much as they wanted to, because in the end, it didn't matter if a girl was a virgin when she married anymore. Marriages didn't last. Love didn't last. Everything fell apart eventually.

Natasha probably appreciated the virgins more than any man did.

However, she didn't like to kill them. It sickened her every time she did it, but it was necessary. She couldn't walk around as a rotting corpse. She would be walking around, still looking for blood, for she could never die.

In her attempts to try to avoid the killings, she even stole used tampons and tried to make an elixir, but it didn't work at all. In fact, the half-assed attempts at creating potions did more harm than good.

There was one time that one of her breasts had nearly fallen right off when she immersed herself in a potion created from living teenagers. Luckily, she had been able to salvage the situation by recognizing that she had to follow the rules Marianne had set forth so very long ago.

The virgins had to die.

Maybe it had to do with their life force. She

didn't know, and she never would know, so it wasn't worth worrying about.

It would be nice to meet another vampire. Someone who understood her constant cravings and how when she wasn't obsessed with hunger, she tried to help other people.

Even the dead.

She looked over at several spirits hovering in the corner, watching her. A new shimmering face was there.

Sandy.

Growing tired of the computer, she decided to set some thoughts down in her diary. She needed to keep a record of all these little piddly details of her life, for though she remembered everything now, she didn't know when the memories would slip away.

Savanna's spell wasn't perfect, but nothing ever was. How could anything created by humans ever be perfect? There was always a balance, a price to be paid for an action or reaction.

Another price Savanna may or may not have been aware of was that even though most of Natasha's memories faded after 50 or so years, some faded much sooner, and others flashed into her mind like sparks with images for fleeting seconds. It didn't matter what the memories were. The coming and going of them was entirely random.

Ideas in her diaries may have been memory, become memory or maybe they never happened at all.

Maybe some of the memories she recorded were only ideas she once had. Or even dreams. Or worse, wishful thinking.

She poised her pen above the paper, recounted the

most recent of her virgin spells and noted improvements in her flesh and spirit.

When the entry was finished, she flipped back through the pages, glancing at words here and there as she searched through her past. She wondered if she had recorded the household ghosts at all. She was certain they hadn't always been there, and she wasn't sure how many were coming and going.

It was time to acknowledge them and remember who they were. She should try to keep track of who came and went and determine if there was any specific reasoning or even astrological significance or patterns.

Sandy was her newest addition. Recently slaughtered Pete came and went a few times, likely because his murder was unsolved. There were many men and, of course, the young women who'd provided her with beauty haunting her, but most of the time she never even knew their names.

Most of them were there haunting her, specifically. Reminding her of what she was. But the others, like Pete, wandered in, maybe looking for a party.

"What do you want from me?" she asked them aloud. The forms shifted and swirled. A young woman floated forward.

"We want you to stop what you're doing. It's wrong."

"I can't stop. I would if I could. You think I don't want to die?"

"You're evil," a young man wailed. "You're selfish and cold."

"I can't help what I am. I do what I can," Natasha said. "I'm sorry you're dead because of me, but it's survival of the fittest. I need something and I take it. Tell me you wouldn't do the same."

"Yet there are people to whom you give so much. What did I ever do to you?" a brown-haired lady cried. "I didn't even know you."

"I'm sorry. I'm truly sorry," Natasha said, her eyes brimming with tears. "I don't like what I am. I try not to kill, I really do. But I hunger. You don't understand."

"Now we hunger too, with you," wailed the woman.

"So be it," Natasha said and returned to her diary. The moaning continued, but Natasha kept writing. She recorded the conversation and slapped the book shut.

"Now you're in here too. One day, people will find out what I am. If they're smart, they'll burn me at the stake. I'm sure I can burn," Natasha said grumpily. She marched into the kitchen and poured cranberry juice into a large, black glass. As she went into the living room, she was glad to see the ghosts had gone elsewhere. Probably to amass a ghost army.

She chuckled as a book flew off the shelf. Then another. As she stood up to put them back, all the books from the top shelf shot out like pellets and landed in a heap on the carpet.

"Wonderful," Natasha said as she kneeled down to scoop them up. "Ellie will be here soon. Thanks, guys."

A few knickknacks flew off the lower shelf and smashed onto the floor.

As she picked up the pieces, she muttered, "Less for Ellie to deal with. Again, thanks, guys."

She swept up the remaining shards and threw

them out. No sooner was she pulling out her dusting cloths than the doorbell rang.

She buzzed Ellie up and opened her door. As she finished organizing the cleaning supplies, Ellie came in, snow falling off her in soft clumps.

"It's bad out there today," she said as she pulled off her boots. Natasha took her coat and hung it on the shower curtain rod in the bathroom.

When she returned, Ellie was looking at the pile of books on the floor.

"Oh, that." Natasha smiled. "We must have had an earthquake. A whole shelf of them fell off."

Ellie looked up at the shelf. "Just one shelf?"

"Yep. Weird, huh?" Natasha said.

"No, just ghosts. There are some here, but you know that. You're the medium."

"Yes, there are some that come and go. Sometimes it's like Grand Central Station."

"It's an old town. There's lots of energy at work here."

"And that's what you're here for. To change the energy."

And get rid of these ghosts.

"Well, let's get started."

As before, Ellie pulled out Gwen's charts and noted where the planets were placed in Natasha's house. She compared it to her *feng shui* grid and then drew up the room.

They rearranged the dining room and living room a bit. There were too many bookcases and heavy pieces of furniture for them to move. They would need help, but, in the end, Ellie decided it was workable.

"What you need in here is plants. Lots of plants.

158

You can have ivy growing along your bookcases. Some green for growth."

"I'm no good with plants. Look, I bought that little tree just before New Year's and already it's dead." Natasha pointed to the husk in the corner.

"That's so sad. Maybe you just don't know how to water it properly."

"I always follow the directions exactly as written. I even have a special watering can."

"Some people are just lousy with plants."

"You can say that again."

Ellie walked around the room, rearranging a few of the gemstones and placing Natasha's large crystal ball higher up on a shelf.

"Well, let's sage it while I think about crystals and gemstones and such." Natasha retrieved her sage stick from the little altar by her desk.

As they walked around the room, they chanted and hummed. The smoke wafted up from the sage stick, filling the room with a thick, sweet smell. Natasha saw the ghosts recoiling from the smell of the herb.

"Be gone, spirits," Natasha called out. "Haunt me no more."

When they had finished walking around the room, Ellie doused the stick in the bowl of sand.

"Okay. I know what to do now. The black and burgundy is overpowering. I know you like it all gothy and stuff, but you need more earthy tones. Browns, tans and greens. Maybe a few throw pillows. Lord knows, you'll never part with your drapes."

"Try me. I'm sick of being haunted. I'll try anything."

"More living, less dead. Look at those morose pictures you have hanging around here. All those depressed Waterhouse maidens luring men to their deaths. You need happy pictures. Lovers and animals."

"Good Lord." Natasha sighed. "Animals? Should I print out some LOL cats and hang them on the walls?"

Ellie laughed. "No. There are lots of classic paintings you can get that aren't depressing."

"Okay, because I draw the line at slogans."

"Nothing to fear, Natasha. You are who you are."

* * *

After Ellie left, Natasha had measured her windows and ordered drapes online from the department store down the street. Now she looked around the room and was relieved to see there were no ghosts. With glee, she ran over to her couch and scooped up the book she had been reading.

It was so nice to have the place to herself again.

Natasha sat on her couch, staring at her new green drapes. Why did they feel so garish? Perhaps the color was too bright for her sensitive eyes.

She resisted the urge to tear them down and decided to give them a week. Maybe by then she'd hear from Gus. He still hadn't answered her email. Now she didn't even have jam sessions with Craig to look forward to anymore.

The new crystal hangings in the window sparkled in the glare of the streetlights from down below. They reflected off the walls and the glass of the new paintings Natasha had found.

She decided to go with framed posters of old movies and chose *West Side Story, Romeo and Juliet* and *Gone with the Wind* as well as a few smaller placards.

Her apartment felt like a vintage store.

She went into her bedroom. At least she didn't feel out of place there yet. She had saged it and, so far, the ghosts seemed to be staying away.

Her mind was racing. What a day it had been. It had started with a phone call from that Bob guy. He wanted her to go over to read for him. He'd sounded so nervous that she almost didn't take the job. But a job was a job, and who was she to decide whether or not he was allowed to communicate with a dearly departed person? His intentions could be pure, for all she knew.

Still, something about it all didn't seem right.

Then she had gone through the ordeal of picking up the curtains and actually hanging them. What a pain in the ass that had been. She was sure her friends would have killed themselves laughing had they seen her climbing up on the window ledges to push the drape brackets in place.

She had bought some colorful green-and-yellow throw pillows and a tan afghan for the couch. She also purchased more gemstones, cleansed them and placed them in strategic corners. She even threw out the poor dead tree and replaced it with an artificial jade plant made from silk.

Ellie had left her *feng shui* charts and Gwen's astrology charts with Natasha. Natasha had poured over them, trying to find even more little things she could do to activate her love energy and be rid of the ghosts. She bought several pieces of rose quartz and hid them in every love corner of every room.

By the time she had finished all her shopping, rearranging, pounding nails into the wall and fiddling with the stones, she was mentally exhausted. She lay back on the bed and thought about Gus. Why hadn't he answered her email? He was the one who had asked her out. She had accepted. Was he so surprised at her agreement? Why couldn't he just pick a date? Men were so weird.

Closing her eyes, she imagined his face in front of her. That mysterious, troubled, strong-jawed, dark-eyed face.

How handsome he was. So broad and muscular. She ached to feel his arms around her again. She dreamed about how his kisses had been so gentle, so soft.

She ran her hands along her breasts, imaging him touching her. How he would kiss her from her neck to her ears, from her cheek to her forehead. His strong fingers would part her legs and rub her pussy firmly.

Natasha pulled off her pants and panties, lay back down and spread her legs. Her fingers touched her swollen clit as she thought about Gus touching her there. She rubbed herself, imagining his hot breath on her neck. How he would tweak her nipple and pull at her breasts. She arched her back so she could slide her fingers into her pussy. Her heat surprised her, and she pushed her fingers in deeper as she imagined them to be his cock.

She pushed against her hand, enjoying the tingling sensations as she stroked herself harder and faster.

It was Gus's cock she was fucking; it was Gus's lips she was kissing.

She rolled over onto her stomach, keeping her hands between her legs. As she pushed herself against the bed, she imagined Gus flipping her onto her hands and knees to fuck her doggy-style. She imagined his big cock slamming into her, pushing her into the bed until he finally came.

Her muscles clamped around her hand, and she climaxed with a groan.

She lay panting for a moment, thoughts of Gus retreating from her mind as sleep overtook her.

Chapter Fourteen

Beware of strangers.

Capture

As Natasha climbed the wooden stairs that led to the front door, a thought flashed through her mind.

There are no ghosts here.

She shrugged off the idea, as she had so many other times when she was called to strange, creepy houses. How many times had Maggie warned her not to go to clients' houses alone?

Natasha shook her head and slapped the large clapper against the door. She stood on the porch, hugging her coat tightly around herself as she tried to hide behind the porch swing from the chilly wind.

Within minutes, Bob, the man from the flea market, opened the door.

"Come in, Miss Natasha," he said, indicating the front hallway. There were mounds of clutter everywhere, from the front hall and into the living room—piles of clothes, boots, fishing tackle and Lord knew what else as far as the eye could see

"Probably messier than what you're used to. I

can't afford servants, and I don't have a wife," he said. "My wife passed. That's why you're here."

"Of course," Natasha said as she picked her way through the home. The locket on her chest burned so hot that she could feel it through her shirt.

A wife. Maggie had said he had asked about his father.

He led her into a room with a wooden table and two chairs. There were three candles to light the whole room.

"It's a bit dark. Can't afford much in the way of candles," he said.

"I understand," Natasha said as she gingerly sat down. She put her purse on the floor beside her. "Candles are good for talking to the spirits."

He sat down in the chair across from her. "I want to talk to her. Really talk to her," he said, his eyes glittering in the darkness.

"We can," Natasha reassured him. "Just close your eyes."

She shut her eyes and waited for the dead wife to come forth. There was nothing.

Just a dark sense of urgency.

A noise swirled in her head. A warning.

She realized she should leave, but it was too late. There was only darkness.

* * *

When she woke, she realized she must be in a basement. She tried to stand but hit her head on steel. Many candles lit the dingy room, and she discovered she was in a cage. Across from her, the man from the

165

flea market snored lightly. There wasn't much else in the room besides the couch Bob lay on and the cage. A table. A couple of chairs.

She pulled at the bars, but they held firm. She ran her fingers along the cold steel trying to find a latch, but there was none. Her locket was gone. She saw it glinting over on the table.

Realizing she was trapped, she let out an unearthly howl.

The sound raised the man from his sleep.

"What the fu…?" he said as he turned his gaze towards her. "Oh, I see you're awake." He shook himself and stood up. "A vampire. My God. Who knew?"

He laughed as Natasha's rage boiled within her.

"What do you want from me? I've done nothing to you," she screamed.

The man stopped and stared at her. "Does William McKenzie ring a bell?"

Natasha stared blankly at him.

"No? Of course not. Why would you get to know the people who keep you alive?" Bob said angrily.

When Natasha didn't answer, he continued on, his voice choking with emotion. "He was my father. Not perfect, but the only one I had."

"I'm sorry," Natasha said.

"No, you aren't. Your kind aren't."

"I really…I mean, I don't kill…"

"Well, you did. He was so shamed, so traumatized…" Bob's voice cracked.

"Why? Because of who he was or what I was?"

"It all came out. The clubs. The other women. He was so riddled with guilt. And my mom…her heart was broken. Why couldn't you leave him alone?"

166

"I don't even know what you're talking about."

"No one knew. No one knew until you came along. When they found him so sick...he confessed to it all. For years. His whole marriage was a lie." The man sobbed.

Natasha watched him coldly. "So why is it my fault he led a double life?"

The man stood up and approached her cage. "You don't get it, do you? If you hadn't hurt him, he'd never have confessed."

"I didn't kill him. It's not my fault. He shouldn't have been where he was without his wife. And he certainly should never have gone home with another woman."

The man sat down heavily on his chair. "I know. I think that too. But still, our lives were perfect before you came along. We had money. Lots of money. Now there's none."

"That's not my fault."

"Oh, but it is, and you're going to pay."

"What do you want? I don't have much money," Natasha said.

"I want you. I want you gone. I know how to do it. I've been waiting for you for five years, until the planets were aligned exactly right. That's when you are the weakest and I'm the strongest. I've done my research. That day is very soon."

"Today is no different than any other," Natasha scoffed. "You can't hurt me."

"Yes, today is different. The next day is different again. It doesn't matter what you think, I'm the one in charge. I know I will triumph."

Natasha watched him. He paced, and his forehead

glistened with sweat. She sat back in her cage. His fear was the thickest scent she could sense. Above him, spirits were gathering.

In amazement, she realized they were whispering about her. *How to help me.*

They didn't want their link to the human race to be destroyed.

It would be a while before he would be able to put his thoughts together enough to do anything with her. In the meantime, she wondered if anyone would notice she was missing.

When she awoke again, he was staring at her. All the lights in the basement were on, and he wore a white gown. She was grateful that she still wore her clothes.

"What do you want?" she asked.

He grinned as he reached toward her. "Your hair is so pretty. I've always wanted to touch it. Can I touch it?" he asked, grabbing onto a clump that fell through the bars.

"Let go," she said.

He jerked his hand back, causing her to press her face against the bars. "No, I won't. I love you, Natasha." He tried to kiss her, but she bared her teeth, tearing his lip.

"Fuck," he cried, sitting back. He held his mouth as blood spilled through his hand. "You like the taste of me, bitch?"

"What answer do you want?" she replied, wiping her mouth with her hand. "I'm sure I don't taste half as vile as you do."

"My blood is the best. And you'll never have it."

"I just did."

"You know what I mean."

He stood up and paced. He sobbed and paced, staring furtively over at her.

"This isn't how I meant it, Natasha." He stopped and stood in front of the cage. "I mean, I like you."

"Oh, please."

"No, really."

"No, you want to kill me. You told me yourself."

"I want to kill vampires. You're evil. But you, Natasha, I love you."

"I am vampire. What do you need to know?"

"I need—I need to know you love me too."

Natasha laughed. "Why would I love you? Tell me, why? I don't even know you."

"But I know you. I've followed you. I've seen you. I've listened to you play the violin. Will you play for me now?"

Natasha stared in disbelief as he brought her violin to her. "How did you get that?"

"Easy. I went into your house and took it."

Anger surged through her. She pulled at the bars in a rage. "You went into my house? That's not fair," she cried.

"You killed my dad, remember? That's not fair."

"I didn't kill your dad. I've not killed anyone for… for…" She couldn't remember. She knew she must have killed someone at some point, even virgins for her youth, but she didn't remember. Yes, she did remember. There was Sandy only just the other day. He was right, she was evil.

"It doesn't matter anymore, Natasha," he said hopefully. "Here, just play your violin."

"How the hell can I play when I'm in a cage?" she asked angrily. "You're crazy."

169

"Crazy for you," he said. "Crazy for your dark, mysterious eyes and your full, red lips."

"Stop it."

"I will."

Before Natasha realized what was happening, he had plunged a hypodermic needle into her hip. He pushed the plunger, and Natasha felt icy coldness running through her veins.

There was blackness once more.

* * *

When Natasha woke again, bright fluorescent lights stung her eyes. She wore heavy chains on her feet, but she was free from the cage. There was nothing around her within reach. The cellar was empty except for her and the shackles around her ankles. There was a small casement window on the far wall. Although there was a ratty curtain over it, she saw shadows on the other side.

Bob watched her from a safe distance on the stairs.

"Now you'll play for me," he said as he picked up the violin and bow from beside him on the stairs.

"Yes, I'll play for you." She sighed as she took her violin. She placed it under her chin and slid the bow along the strings. A mournful sound wailed from her fingertips as she played. The music filled the room, and soon the man grew teary-eyed.

"Play something happier," he finally said.

"I'm not your puppet. You're lucky I'm playing at all," she retorted, vibrating her fingers into a rich, luxurious vibrato.

"You are so beautiful when you play," he said.

She stopped and glared at him. "Silence. Or I will play no more."

"Very well," he said

She played, losing herself in the rich, fantastic tones that echoed through the room. Her mind was blank as her fingers danced along the fingerboard. She wasn't in a basement. She wasn't at a concert. She was inside the notes, humming and vibrating.

Around them, the ghosts ebbed along the walls, watching and waiting, rolling their ethereal heads in time to her slow, undulating rhythm.

The shadows in the casement window seemed to grow larger and then fade. When she finally finished, she handed the violin back to the man.

"There, I played for you. Now will you let me go so I can get back to work?"

"Oh no, Natasha. There's no way I can let you go now. You might tell on me," he said as he stomped up the stairs with the violin.

"Let me go," she roared, pulling at the shackles on her legs.

"No," replied the distant voice.

"I want my necklace back," she screamed.

"You can't have it. God knows what spells you'd cast on me," he shouted.

"Damn you," she cried. She looked around the room. There had to be something she could use to escape the locks.

As she crawled around, she became aware of a chemical smell permeating the room. Within seconds, she was asleep again.

When she woke once more, she was shackled to a

wall. The man stood in front of her, his lips twitching nervously into a smile.

"My beautiful Natasha. You're awake," he said kindly. He reached over to push her hair back from her face. She spit at him. "Now, now. You must remain ladylike."

She tried to talk but realized he had placed a plastic ball gag into her mouth.

"You're still pretty, but you just can't answer back," he said. "Or bite me." He stroked one of her breasts through the thin cotton of her blouse. "Very nice. I really think we can get to know each other now."

He fondled both her breasts. Natasha fought against the restraints, but they held her tight. In the far corner, several ghosts huddled, watching the scene unfold. To the side was the grieving face of a man. His energy spilled into her, and she stared at him. It was William McKenzie.

His message was to his son.

Natasha couldn't say anything, so she closed her eyes. She willed the father to be gone, but when she opened her eyes, he was still there. Another face joined him. Another person who had died by her hand.

She struggled against the shackles as Bob ran his hands between her legs.

"You are my beauty, my queen. I can cure you, you know." He stepped back proudly and went over to small table he had set up while she was sleeping.

He held out a cup of liquid. The stench from it turned her stomach.

"Don't worry. You don't have to drink it. I heard this elixir would cure any vampire. I got it at the flea market. A man was selling it."

Natasha watched the spirits swirl over Bob. The shadows at the window flickered back and forth.

Bob approached her with the steaming brew. The foul smell made Natasha dizzy.

As Bob held the cup to pour the elixir over her head, there was a crashing from the window. The glass blew inward, and a large, clawed hand groped inside. The sound startled Bob, and much of the mixture slopped out over Natasha. She screamed as it seared through her, puffs of steam rising from her burning flesh. Droplets of it splashed into her eyes, and she squeezed them shut, the burning beginning in her left eye and rapidly blurring her vision.

Bob stared with horror as a large man-beast wriggled through the window. The creature was muscular and covered in a thick mat of blond hair. Massive, furry hands slapped the potion from Bob and sent it flying onto the floor. The spirits shrank back into the corners as the enormous beast stood in front of Bob.

"What the fuck are you?" Bob cried out, staring at the huge, gnashing jaws that dripped with drool.

The wolf-man whacked Bob into a corner with one hand and loped over to the screaming Natasha. She cried as the acid burned into her, searing her flesh from her bones. The skin on her face was melting; her hair fell out in clumps.

Bob moaned from the floor, struggling to get up as the wolf-man easily tore away the leather straps that held Natasha. As the wolf-man tried to hold her up, Bob scrambled to his feet and jumped onto the wolf-man's back.

"Don't free her. She's evil. She's a vampire."

The wolf-man turned and tore at him with his clawed hand. The flesh on Bob's face easily ripped away, exposing his jaw and cheekbone. Bob screamed as the wolf-man tackled him to the ground. Natasha fell over, going unconscious; the last sounds she heard were Bob's screams as the beast pulled him apart.

Chapter Fifteen

Your friends define who you are.

Natasha's Recovery

Natasha woke in a bed in the circle room of Lucy's house. Every bone in her body ached. Her hunger was enormous, and she sat up too quickly. She lay back down dizzily and stared around her.

The women were all there. They watched her from their spots in the circle, eyes staring worriedly from under hooded robes. Candles flickered, and the smell of frankincense was strong.

Natasha saw there was a man there too. She sat up again, recognizing Jim Hawthorne. "You," she said, pointing weakly. "You…"

She sank back down into her pillows. What was Jim Hawthorne doing there? Why was he in the circle?

She felt warmth on her chest, and, looking down, she saw the locket was back around her neck. It glowed with an unearthly hue.

Lucy stepped forward and took Natasha's hand.

"We thought we lost you," she said, her eyes glistening with tears. "What happened?"

Strange fragments of memory returned to her. A basement. The ghosts watching. Playing the violin. Bob. The wolf-man.

She sat up again.

"Is Bob…?"

"Yes, Bob is dead. We found him, or rather, what was left of him. We took care of it. Don't worry."

"How did you find me?"

"It doesn't matter right now. How are you feeling?" Lucy asked, stroking Natasha's hair.

"Not so good. Is my face…?"

"Your face is fine. We've been working on you for the past week. Spells and potions. Bringing you back."

"I'm so grateful. To all of you."

"It was Jim who was the most help," Lucy said as she waved Jim over.

"It was? How?"

Lucy cleared her throat. "Jim is a vampire hunter."

Natasha flinched.

Lucy laughed. "But not in a bad way, dearie, or you wouldn't be here."

Jim stepped over to her. "I've been studying vampires my whole life. Watching how they feed and how they live. Trying to understand the science of how they work. How you work."

"Why?"

"I don't know why. A calling, I guess. I've always been fascinated by vampires, and as a child, I thought they were just a story. But eventually, I realized they were real. To make along story short, I was able to help the ladies create a way to save you.

176

The charts from Gwen, the spells from Lucy, pages from your diaries…"

"My diaries…" Natasha said.

"Don't worry," Lucy said. "It was only Jim and I going through them, looking for clues on how to help you." She leaned forward and whispered into Natasha's ear. "You are young and beautiful once more."

Natasha grinned. "You don't hate me?"

Lucy laughed. "Of course we don't hate you. We love you, Natasha. We've all been here for you. Your secret is safe with us."

* * *

Natasha moved into one of Lucy's big bedrooms while she recovered. The days blended together at first, a hazy blur of trying to regain her strength.

One day, as she sat reading, there was a knock at the door.

"Come in," she said.

The door opened and Gus stepped in, clutching a bouquet of black roses. He grinned when he saw her. "You look so much better now."

"How did you know I was here?" she asked.

"Don't worry about that. How are you feeling?"

"Much better now that you're here."

Gus sat on the edge of her bed and took her hand.

"I'm sorry I ran off on you that day. I…I had something that needed to be taken care of."

"That's all right."

"I would like very much to see you again, when you're better."

"I would like that, too," Natasha said. She breathed in his scent deeply as they chatted about nothing. She stared at his face and his hands, yearning to touch and kiss him.

"You must rest so that you can return home," he said, kissing her on the forehead.

"Thank you for coming to visit me," Natasha said.

So many images played through her mind, a lifetime of pictures, of struggles, of pain. Flashes of flying fur, of blood and cages haunted her. She often thought about how she had been carried through the woods and snow in the arms of a giant beast. She had been terrified that one monster was being traded for another, yet she woke up under the care of Lucy.

She dreamed of being stronger so that she could see Gus again. She ached for him more with each passing hour.

She stared over at her beloved violin, safe in its case and relieved that the witches had found it for her. Her fingers itched to dance across the strings.

She couldn't wait until she was strong once more.

Finally, she was able to return home.

The first thing she did was go to her music room and play her violin. It was the best homecoming she could have asked for, playing her music by herself.

After she played, she decided to go for a walk. Maybe she would go over to the woods if the snow wasn't too deep along the paths. She hadn't been over there in a long time.

Chapter Sixteen

You may meet your soul mate.

The Woods

The woods were darker with every step away from the moonlight. Even the glow of the snow was eventually lost as Natasha crept along the path. She kept gloved hands out to catch the passing branches and picked her way carefully across icy patches.

The hum continued.

It was madness to continue this venture into the unknown, yet the noise tickled her under her skin.

At last she saw an orange glow in the distance. As she drew closer, the glow became flickering, crackling flames. A small fire spat and burned, illuminating darkness at the mouth of a cave.

The humming was coming from inside.

Natasha stood watching the fire. She waited, knowing there was something around her. She closed her eyes, and labored breathing filled her mind. *He* was waiting for her. Whoever *he* was. Masculine and strong. Calling her.

She opened her eyes again with confidence and moved forward. She passed the fire and stood before the mouth of the cave. The humming stopped, and now the breathing had moved from her mind to hot breath warming her face. She turned to run, but something large grabbed her arm with a force that spun her back. She was clamped tightly to a large, furry chest. Pinned, she was unable to struggle, and let herself be taken to wherever it was they were going to go.

His grip was strong as he loped through underground mazes. Eventually, Natasha passed out from his relentless clutching and dreamed of blackness.

When she finally woke, she stared around the room in dazed wonderment. She was still wearing her clothes as she sat up in a large four-poster bed. Dozens of electric candles lit the room. There was a bookcase filled with books, a boom box, and several large crystals. A giant poster of the solar system with various astrological markings handwritten in various colors was on one of the far walls.

There were two chairs, and a huge, hairy beast sat in one of them, staring into a crystal ball. He turned his head, and she gasped when she saw his face.

He was Gus but not Gus. Somehow, he was a wolf, a bear, a man. His features blended into each other, yet he was still striking. *Charismatic?* His eyes locked onto her own. Gus's eyes.

"You're awake." It was a statement made in a gravelly growl.

Natasha cringed. "Gus? Why have you called me here?"

"I needed you...to see." He stood up, and she gasped at his size. Long, dark fur hung from his already huge frame. A leather pouch dangled around

180

his neck. His hands were paw-like claws, as were his feet. His cock dangled firmly between his legs.

"See?" Natasha said as she stared at his cock. "I see…wow." She shook her head.

"Natasha. It's not funny," he said as he approached her, his teeth bared in a snarl.

"Oh…" she said. "I didn't mean…I mean…I'm impressed. By all of it. Are you a werewolf?"

"What do you think?"

"How?"

Gus turned away from her and began to pace the room in a circle. "About five years ago, I was in England. I was hanging out around Stonehenge. I wasn't supposed to be, but I was. I was attacked."

"Did you turn right away?"

His pacing quickened, his hands clenching and unclenching. "Immediately. It was ugly. But I've learned to control it." He pointed to his crystals. "They're from around the world. I put them on my chakras. I'm able to sort of control my urges like that."

"Really?"

"Not all the time. Only when the planets are right. See here?" He pointed to Venus. "This is a good time for me to use the crystals and try to talk to you. Over here…"He pointed to another spot on the chart. "I have to stay hidden. I'll lock myself in here for a few days."

"No kidding."

"It's freaky. Using astrology to socialize myself. But it's working. With the crystals and some spells."

He turned away.

"It doesn't always work." He paced again. Natasha noted that his cock was growing erect.

"What do you want from me?"

He stood in front of her. "I want to get to know you. But I want you to know the real me first. I thought maybe here in Hermana, someone like you would understand this werewolf business more than someone out in the real world."

"Well, we are more open-minded here," she said. "What do you want to do?"

"I want to touch you," he said.

Natasha stared at the long claws. "I don't know."

"You have clothes on." He reached for her. "Remember how we danced on New Year's Eve?" He clicked on a CD player with a remote. A classical waltz swelled over the sound system.

"Yes, I do," Natasha said and stepped toward him. She closed her eyes and rested her head against his fur.

As they danced, Natasha felt him shifting in her arms. He was changing. By the time the song was over, Gus was human again.

"How did you do that?" she asked.

"I didn't. You did."

"I did?" Natasha returned to the bed and sat down. "I don't understand."

"I don't, either. It has to do with the charts. Sometimes I'm human, sometimes I'm not." He realized he was naked and covered his groin with his hands. "I think I'd better get dressed," he said as he went over to a dresser. He took out a sweater and jeans. Natasha admired the way his back muscles rippled as he bent over to pull on his pants.

Once he was dressed, he stood before her again. "Not so scary now," he said. "Or impressive."

"Gus…is this why you didn't answer my email?"

"That and it's hard to get access to a computer at that Internet café. I don't exactly have electricity here. I'll run the generator now and then, as you heard, but that's it." Gus sat beside her and took her hand. "What do you think? Do you want to try to be with me?"

"Here?" she asked.

"No. I mean, do you want to go out? See where it goes?"

"Yes, I do."

"Even though I am what I am?"

"I don't care. Everyone has their secrets. Maybe we can help each other." She smiled.

"The hunger though. I kill people, you know. I killed Pete."

"I know. I know about killing."

"I know you do, Natasha. I know what you are."

Natasha turned to him in surprise. "How?"

"At first, it was the smell. The death and decay that surrounds you."

"I have that smell?" Natasha frowned. "I always hope to drown it out with all the scented soap I use. I always have incense burning as well."

"It's deeper than that. I'm sure others don't notice. I just have a sensitive nose." He grinned. The candles cast long shadows across his face.

"Okay. I hope so. I'd hate to think I was disgusting my friends."

She leaned over and sniffed him. His masculine scent was mixed with nervous sweat. "I wondered what was different about you," she said. "I could smell something about you too."

"I guess it takes one to know one."

"So, tell me about your hunger. Is it all-consuming?" Natasha asked.

He nodded. "It's like a blackness overcomes me and I can't stop until I've eaten. It's a terrible thing, and I always feel so guilty when I'm me again."

"I know. I have figured out ways to kind of cope. But it still isn't great."

"Tell me," Gus said.

"I pick up strange men in fetish clubs. Men who I think are married. That way they aren't as likely to tell about some strange woman who seduced them and drank their blood. They always keep their mouths shut. Almost always," she said with a sigh. "That Bob guy, I killed his father accidentally. Well, his father killed himself out of embarrassment."

"Oh, so that's why he captured you."

"Yeah, but then he got weirdly attracted to me. Pervert like his dad. He loved it when I was all caged up."

"It takes all kinds."

"It does." Natasha took Gus's hand. "So now what?"

"So now we kiss. Right?" Gus said as he tilted her head toward him. He pressed his lips against hers gently, just like he had on New Year's Eve. Natasha leaned into him, wrapping her arms around the large, broad shoulders she had ached to hug for so long. His kisses grew in intensity, and she kissed back, darting her tongue into his mouth. He pulled back and kissed her neck, her cheek, her hair.

"I've been wanting to kiss you for so long," he said as he kissed her mouth again. "I think about New Year's Eve all the time."

"So do I."

184

They kissed again, their hands stroking each other's backs. They pulled into each other, sharing their warmth as the fire crackled and spat.

Gus pushed her back, holding her tightly, his lips still meeting with hers. She held him close, her body tingling with excitement. He moaned softly as he kissed her, smelling her hair and running his hands along the length of her body. She writhed under his touch, rising up to meet his hands as he stroked her breasts and legs.

He sat up and pulled off his sweater. "It's suddenly very hot in here," he said. "I shouldn't have bothered getting dressed."

"No, you shouldn't have," Natasha said as she slipped off her blouse. She unhooked her bra, and Gus admired her full breasts. He leaned over to take one of her nipples in his mouth. She sighed softly as his tongue flicked back and forth.

Natasha rubbed Gus's chest and arms with her hands. The firm sensation of his muscular flesh was pleasing as she stroked him. Her hands reached down to his ass, and she squeezed it, pulling him against her. She wrapped her legs around him, her still-clothed groin yearning to feel him inside of her.

Gus held her breasts, alternately kissing first one and then the other. He licked her nipples, teasing them with his lips. Natasha moaned.

"Oh, Gus. That feels so nice."

He took a nipple into his mouth, sucking it until it was a firm peak. He nibbled it with his teeth, grazing it lightly. The feeling made her quiver with delight.

His hands reached down to her pants and unsnapped them. She let him slide them off. She wriggled back on the bed in delicious anticipation. She was aching to feel him inside her.

He kneeled down beside the bed and leaned over to lick her pussy. He pulled open her pussy lips until his tongue found her tingling clit. The first lick sent chills down her back. She spread her legs wider, and he licked her again.

"More," she urged. "Oh, more."

He flicked his tongue on her clit, pressing it softly, then flicking it rapidly. She squirmed under his skill and fondled her own breasts.

"That feels so good. Oh my God," she groaned.

He slid two fingers into her pussy while his tongue continued to lick her. His fingers hooked into her, finding her G-spot. She bucked her hips up to meet his tongue, to encourage him to push his fingers in deeper and deeper.

"Faster," she cried out, her legs trembling as she shivered with anticipation. The pressure was building the faster he finger-fucked her. His tongue continued to dance, and she eagerly enjoyed him.

Just as she was about to come, she realized someone had entered the room.

Gus jerked up and snapped his head around at the same time Natasha sat up. Jim Hawthorne stood there, a gun in his hand and a smirk on his face.

"Oh my, what have we here?" Jim said. "A werewolf and a vampire. What a lovely couple."

Natasha scrambled to the end of the bed, pulling up the bedclothes. "What do you want?" she cried out.

"I want to stop the madness, is what I want," Jim said. "Both of you. No good at all. A vampire can be trained, however. A beast cannot."

186

"What are you talking about? Why do you have a gun? You saved me, remember?" Natasha asked.

"Yes, I saved you for Lucy, you despicable creature. It's only because of Lucy that you still live. However, Lucy won't be hurt if Gus is destroyed. She doesn't know him."

Natasha's eyes widened as Jim pointed the gun at Gus. Before anyone could say anything, Jim pulled the trigger. There was a loud blast, and Gus collapsed to the floor.

"Oh my God, Gus!" Natasha cried as she leapt off the bed to go to him. He lay unconscious, blood pooling from a wound in his chest. "You better not have killed him," she sobbed.

"But, indeed, I hope I have," Jim said smugly. He put the gun back into his jacket. "It's a silver bullet. He's done."

Jim turned to leave, and Natasha lunged for him. "You bastard," she screamed as she tackled him. "How dare you! I loved him."

Jim wrestled with her, trying to push her from him, and they fell to the floor.

"Of course, every woman loves her knight in shining armor. When he's the knight. Sure, Gus saved you from that crazy man, but he has killed a lot of people. Face the facts, Natasha. He would reveal your secret sooner or later."

"No, he wouldn't have. " Natasha pinned Jim to the floor. She pressed his arms down, her eyes blazing. Her strength intensified as her rage surged through her.

"How dare you take him from me?" she screamed.

"Let me up, Natasha. It's better this way."

187

"No!" she cried. With a roar, she leaned down toward him and tore a mouthful of flesh from his neck. He screamed as the blood poured out of the gaping hole. Natasha reached down again, and this time she latched on. She drank hungrily and fully for the first time in decades as his fists pressed against her strong grip. He bucked and wriggled, but her strength was greater.

His screaming and kicking soon ebbed, and finally, he stopped moving.

Natasha continued to feed until she could feed no more. When she had finally drained enough from him, she sank back against the bed.

"Oh my God," she wept. She wiped her blood-smeared mouth with her hand. "What have I done? What has he done? Oh God. Oh Gus."

Natasha's bloated and full belly sloshed and gurgled as she crawled over to where Gus lay. He was still, lifeless, cold.

She opened his shirt and saw the silver bullet glinting in his chest through the meat of his bloody wound.

With a shriek, she collapsed on top of him, sobbing uncontrollably.

Chapter Seventeen

Healing brings freedom.

Natasha Goes to See Lucy

Gus lay on a cot in the middle of the circle, naked except for a cloth draped over his groin. There were chunks of amber, citrine and tourmaline on the floor as well as quartz and rose quartz. Candles and incense burned. Around him, 12 hooded friends prayed for his recovery.

His chest was bandaged where Lucy had removed the bullet earlier.

"He's not dead yet. We got him in time," Lucy had said when she examined the bullet. "Jim did nice work. Right down to the symbols." She placed the bullet into a bowl. "The bullet paralyzes him for a while, but we may be able to save him if we can get him revived before the poison takes hold. Unlike you, he's not eternal. Call the others while I put a poultice on him."

Within hours, the circle had been formed. All with the exception of Gwen, who was flying through China that night. Everyone was eager to help Gus. Even Maggie was able to get there in a timely manner.

The women arrived solemnly and focused all their energy on helping their new friend.

"Let's call upon the spirits of a higher power to come down and fill Gus with the life force," Lucy called out to the air. "Everyone focus on sending healing energy to Gus."

The women chanted foreign words, staring intently at Gus. Natasha said the words, trying to put meaning into them, but she was so numb that she wasn't even sure if her mouth was working.

If Gus was dead, she wanted to forget him. She wanted to forget all they could have been if only he had lived.

The women sang several songs as the candles burned and the incense smoldered. Ellie and Adele kept bursting into tears as they sang along with the others. The mood of the room was beyond depressing. The worst part was the sorrowful stares from Lily and Ursula. Natasha didn't know if she could stand to be *that woman* whose lover was murdered.

The humming and singing seemed to drone on forever. Natasha kept staring at Gus, as if her stares alone could bring him back.

At last, Lucy closed the circle.

Quietly, the women hugged Natasha good-bye, and soon everyone was gone. The room seemed so empty and Gus seemed so small and lost.

"Oh, Lucy…it didn't work."

"No, it doesn't seem as though it did, does it?" Lucy said.

"I never even really got a chance to get to know him. I never even…" Natasha sobbed as Lucy put her arms around her.

190

"Wait," Lucy said. "Oh my! In all the flurry, I forgot one more thing that just might help."

"What is it? I'll do anything. Anything at all," Natasha said.

"The locket. We must use the locket. Of course."

Natasha took it off and handed it to Lucy. "There. Use it."

Lucy waved the locket over one of the burning pots of incense and then walked over to Gus. She held the locket over him, closing her eyes and whispering words Natasha couldn't hear. Lucy muttered and hummed while Natasha stared expectantly at Gus.

"Is it working?" Natasha asked. Lucy shook her head. She placed the locket over Gus's heart, where the wound was bandaged. She stepped away and stood beside Natasha.

"That's the best I can do. That's the best anyone can do," Lucy said. "I'm sorry, dear." She patted Natasha on the cheek and headed out of the room.

Natasha stood over Gus and closed her eyes. She willed his heart to start beating, for his lungs to fill with air, for his eyes to open and see her waiting for him.

When she opened her eyes again, the locket was glowing. Around her, ghostly forms whirled. They were her ghosts and other ghosts. Spirits from hundreds of years of life in Hermana and the world flooded into the room. They floated, weaving in and out of each other in a wave of ribbons. The vision reminded Natasha of a braided basket.

As the ghosts connected and swirled, a circle formed in the air around Gus. Natasha was aware of a new surge of energy. The ghosts twittered and hummed light, tinkling sounds, like glass wind chimes.

Natasha watched as the locket grew brighter. She could almost feel heat emitting from it. She laid her hands on Gus and focused on the light energy beaming down from the sky and through her fingers. She didn't know if reiki worked for vampires and werewolves, but she had watched it enough to know what to do. Her fingers grew warm as she focused. She willed the light into Gus, hoping it would be enough to bring him back.

The whirling above her grew faster. A light wind swept through the room, and Pete's essence soared through. He floated above Gus for a moment, an anguished look on his face. With an unearthly moan, he flew toward Gus and tunneled into him. Natasha waited for him to emerge, but he never did.

The ghosts above continued to spin, creating almost a vortex. Natasha grew fearful they would create a portal for something even more terrible.

"It's okay," she said. "I think we're done here. We've done all we can."

The ghosts slowly stopped whirring and wafted apart. Many of them floated to different areas of the room to watch while others wandered off to other areas of the house.

Natasha turned her attention back to Gus. His chest was flinching. For a brief moment, she worried Pete would come bursting out of him *Alien*-style, but in fact, Gus started to cough. He coughed hard and long, racking his body so violently that he leaned over to perch himself on his arms.

"Oh my God," he wheezed. He sucked great mouthfuls of air in and out, coughing up clots of blood onto the carpet. "I'm sorry," he said as he wiped his mouth with his hand. "I'm sorry for everything."

Natasha stared at him with joy. "You're back. Oh Gus! I can't believe it."

She hugged him and he held her hard in his embrace. His body shook as his coughing turned to crying.

"What happened, Natasha? I'm so confused."

"You died, Gus. You were shot. But the witches brought you back."

Gus grinned. "Your witch friends, huh? They did that for me?"

"I told you."

"Even knowing what I am?"

"Yes, even knowing what you are. It's all going to be fine now." Natasha grinned. "You'll see."

Chapter Eighteen

Try a new recipe. Experiment with new food.

Natasha and Gus

Natasha led Gus into the bedroom. Gus was glistening from his shower. Natasha was naked, and her body cast long, sexy shadows on the walls. Gus gasped as he saw all the electric candelabras glowing. There were six real candles flickering on the nightstands. The smell of sweet incense filled the air.

"I've waited so long for this," Natasha said as she led Gus toward the bed. "Take me before we're interrupted again."

Gus laughed as he flung off his towel. The mark where he was shot had almost healed in just a few short hours.

"You don't have to ask me twice," he said. He pushed her back on the bed, cradling her face in his hands. "My beautiful Natasha. Together at last. I think." He kissed her on the lips quickly. "I must say, something sure smells good," he said as he raised his head, looking toward the kitchen.

"My horoscope said to try a new recipe today. So I did. While you were in the shower, I made dinner."

"Oh, a woman who cooks. I like that." Gus nibbled her ear.

"Take me, Gus. Oh, take me like you were going to the other night."

Gus kissed her, licking her neck. She tilted her head back so he could nibble along the length of it. His mouth pressed warmly along her jugular, and her heartbeat quickened. His breath grew shorter, and beads of sweat formed on his brow.

Natasha kissed him on the lips again, noting that his face felt a bit rougher. She pushed him back.

"Oh, don't stop kissing me," Gus pouted as he wiped the sweat from his brow. Natasha looked down at his erection. It was growing larger and longer. She leaned over and sucked it into her mouth.

"Oh my God," Gus moaned. "That feels so good."

She licked him along his shaft in long, slow strokes. Her hand cupped his balls, pressing them warmly with her fingers, tugging on them lightly. His cock kept growing as she licked him. She took him in her mouth, opening her throat to slide him all the way in.

"Oh Natasha," he growled, holding her hair in his hands. He pumped her head up and down, gripping her hair firmly. Natasha sucked him, her head bobbing as his hips thrust up to meet her.

He was so big that she couldn't fit the length of him in her mouth. She stroked his erection with one hand while sucking on his tip. He quivered and trembled as excitement grew. His hands were rough in her hair, scratching her.

She looked up at him and noticed the sweat was

pouring down his face in rivulets; his chest gleamed with moisture. Even his neck had a steady stream of perspiration trickling down.

"Are you okay?" she asked, pulling away from his clutch. As he released her hair, they both saw that his hands had turned to claws. He jumped up.

"Oh no," Natasha said. "Now what?"

"This time isn't supposed to be so bad," Gus said, pacing in a circle. "It's the next time I have to hide myself away."

"But aren't you hungry?" Natasha asked.

"I'm always hungry," Gus said.

"Well then, maybe we should eat first. If you think you can."

"It does smell good. But you know what I need to eat."

"I know, darling. However, we are here, and we can only have what is lying around," Natasha said. "Come, let's go eat."

Natasha led Gus into the dining room. She took one of the cloth napkins from the table and gave it to him to dab away his sweat. He was still shifting. Fur grew along his face as his nose and mouth were elongating. His chest grew furrier, and he had claws that could barely hold the napkin. She went into the kitchen.

"Smells good," Gus shouted to her, his voice low and gravelly.

Natasha returned with two plates piled high with slices of rare mea as well as a baked potato and broccoli.

"This looks familiar." Gus smiled as he stared at the food.

"I was hoping you'd remember," Natasha said. She poured red wine for both of them. She placed a black goblet in front of him. "Drink this. It will help you relax."

Gus tried to wrap his claws around the glass, but they didn't bend that way.

"Damn it," he growled.

"Now don't go getting all upset," Natasha said as she went over to him. "I'll help you. It'll be kind of fun."

Natasha took the glass and tipped it to his mouth. He slurped noisily, drinking the wine until it was gone.

"A bit thirsty?" she asked.

"I just thought I'd get it over with so you can go eat," he said rather harshly.

Natasha frowned for a moment. "I really don't mind," she said with forced cheerfulness as she poured more wine into his glass. "I'm here for you, however you need me."

She took his knife and fork and cut a big piece of meat. She raised it to his lips, and he ate it hungrily.

"That is so good," he said. "That really hits the spot."

"Eat it," Natasha coaxed, stabbing the meat as fast as she could to keep up with his vigorous feasting.

At last, he had consumed his plate of meat, and she went to get him another.

"I can't believe how good that is," he called out to her.

"I'm glad you like it," she shouted back.

In the end, he ate three plates of meat to her one. He even ate all of his baked potato and broccoli.

They sat back for a moment, their stomachs full.

Natasha dabbed her mouth with her napkin as she finished the last of her meat.

"Natasha," Gus said. He held up his hands. "Check it out." They weren't claws anymore. "And I've stopped sweating." He smiled. His distorted face had returned back to normal again.

Natasha smiled. "Look at you. You didn't turn."

"I told you I was hungry, and you fed me. It's strange, though. Regular food doesn't turn me back. At least, it hasn't until now. Did you put a spell in it?"

"No, I didn't." She smirked. "But it *was* special."

"In what way?"

"Well…" Natasha tried to speak seriously, but laughter kept threatening to spill from her lips. "Remember Jim Hawthorne? The one that shot you?"

"Yes."

"Well…"She raised her eyebrows.

Gus looked down at his plate and back at her. "You didn't."

"Why not? They were just going to put him in the ground to rot, if they ever found him, that is. Why let the bears have what is rightfully ours?" She sipped her wine.

"You're right, we are going to be good together," he said as he went over to hug her. He kissed her long and hard. She responded hungrily, her heart pounding.

He scooped her up in his arms and carried her back to the bedroom. "Do you think *this* time we can finish what we started?" he asked.

"Oh, I most certainly hope so." She sighed, stroking his jaw.

He lay her gently down on the bed and kissed her. His cock was already hard and ready. She spread her legs and cried out as, at long last, she felt the warmth of his penetration. She raised her hips up to meet him, gasping as his size.

"Oh, Gus," she cried as she pulled him down on top of her.

He plunged into her deeply, and she cried out with joy. He pumped her faster and harder. She wrapped her legs around him, rocking against him.

She rejoiced in their union, enjoying him filling her up at last. Her hunger quelled, she was able to enjoy the glorious sensation of his penetration as she'd not been able to do with any other.

He pulled out of her, and she gasped as the fullness of him left her.

Gus rolled her over and turned her around so she was on her hands and knees. As her breasts swung, he pulled on her hips to draw her back against him. He fucked her slowly and sensuously, kneading her bottom with his fingers. She turned back to look at him, at his rippled chest and strong abdominal muscles tightening as he pumped into her. He smiled at her.

"Do you like that?" he asked as he fucked her.

"Oh, yes. Harder. Faster."

He pushed into her deeply and pulled out again, picking up the pace of his rhythm. His hand rubbed her clitoris, and she moaned as a shuddering thrill passed through her.

He turned her over again, this time lifting her legs up onto his shoulders. As he plunged into her repeatedly, he kissed her. Their tongues met and mingled as their bodies churned together.

His pace grew more frantic, and he tilted her up higher to thrust into her deeper.

"Oh my God," Natasha cried as a climax spread through her. She gasped and shook her head back and forth as he pumped into her faster and harder.

He stiffened, and with a groan, he released into her. Natasha felt him pulsing inside her tight, warm hole, and she came again.

For a while, he stayed inside her as they savored the delicious sensation of their excitement subsiding. Slowly, he pulled out of her and lay down beside her.

They both gasped, catching their breath as they lay staring at the ceiling. "That was amazing," he said.

"Oh yeah," Natasha agreed. She noticed some of the ghosts were hovering above them. They were quiet and seemed almost approving. She turned back to Gus. "I'm glad we found each other. I think we're going to be a good team."

"I think we're going to be just fine," Gus agreed as he pressed his lips against hers.

Excerpt from Aquarius: Haunted Heart
Book Two in the *Witch Upon a Star* Series

Chapter One

Reflecting on your past will help you make wiser choices in the future.

The heat of the sun bore down on her. She squinted, pushing her hands against the broad shoulders of the faceless stranger as his velvet tongue sought out her innermost desire. She spread her legs wider, allowing him deeper access with his fingers and mouth. He slowly ran his tongue along her labia, in and out of her moist folds, until he found her clit again. She moaned and pushed up against him, urging him to suck her hard, little nub. His noisy slurps excited her, and she braced herself for a quick and powerful orgasm.

The alarm clock buzzed.

Madeline slapped it off with a groan. The dream image faded, but her urgent desire didn't. She curled up under the blankets, pressing her groin into the mattress until she made herself come.

Another day had arrived.

* * *

It was a cold February morning as Madeline stared at herself in the mirror. She had just emerged from a hot, pounding shower, and it was the best time to indulge in a bit of self-scrutiny. It was a daily ritual and one she imagined most people in North America performed. But probably unlike most people, after she had her morning glance, she usually didn't bother looking at herself again until the next day. Even when she brushed her teeth, she often stared down into the sink instead of checking out her appearance. She often realized she didn't really look how she felt.

With her birthday just past, Madeline still felt on the inside like a gawky, misinformed teenager. Yet, according to her birth certificate, she was now the ripe old age of 31.

Thirty-one and never married.

Thirty-one and never even engaged.

She had no one to blame but herself.

And in looking into the mirror, she could see that though she didn't look as though she was in her thirties, she was certainly well past the gawky teenager stage of her life.

Now she was a gawky over-thirty-year-old woman.

She wasn't the best-looking girl on the planet, but she wasn't the worst either. Her hips, thighs and stomach were a bit too round for her height. And who was to blame for that?

No one but herself.

Sitting at her desk for hours and hours made her round. Eating chocolate every few minutes helped. Her sugar addiction was going to kill her one day, she was told on a regular basis by the media and by her friends.

Her eyes were steel gray, and she had soft, light brown, wavy hair. She turned sideways, staring at her pendulous breasts and pear-shaped hips. She had to get back to the gym. Jessica, her trainer, was going to kill her for not sticking to it this time.

It just was so hard to get exercise. The endless days sitting at the computer writing articles and books and then the skulking around haunted houses with recording devices didn't give her much time for anything else. Not for exercise. Not for dating.

She sucked in her stomach until it almost was flat. She ran her hand along it, imagining it toned and tanned like a model's. Imagination was all it would ever be. She'd never been that toned in her life, and at 31, she couldn't dream she'd ever have the focus and self-discipline it took to be truly buff.

She huffed out the stale air and ran her hands through her hair, pulling it on top of her head. Maybe if she wore more ponytails, she'd look younger. Leaning closer to the mirror, she peered at the crow's feet lining her eyes. Character. Yes, she had character because she'd been through so much.

No more and no less than anyone else, when she really thought about it. But unlike many others, she hid her wounds deep. Her heart ached constantly until sometimes she thought she couldn't take it anymore.

Why did she ache so much?

She wasn't sure if she believed in love. Real love. A true, faithful love where there was no hurt and no cheating.

She had never truly loved, she didn't think. Not in a romantic-love kind of way.

Sure she had loved her parents, her relatives, puppies and kittens. That kind of love was easy for her. She loved the starving children in Third World countries, the displaced flood victims in New Orleans, the shooting victims in Paris and the orphans from September 11. Her universal unconditional love had no boundaries and no limits.

She loved peace, not war.

But these things were easy to love. These were ideas, abstracts. They were emotions of hope and victory.

But to love another human being, to fully trust another human being with her heart, with her mind, with her body? She didn't know if she was capable of that. She didn't know if any honest and true human was capable of that.

For in her mind, love was an illusion. Love was a word made to be broken.

Falling in love was just one short step from falling into despair. Giving oneself completely to another for a lifetime was against human nature. Logically, no one could truly be committed and satisfied with one other person forever. Could they?

She knew many people in long-term marriages who seemed happy, compatible and complementary. But she often wondered how much of it was a front for people like her watching them, and how much bitterness and despair seeped behind closed doors.

How often was the news full of shocking tragedies perpetrated by people who were so "happy," so "peaceful," so "gentle," and of course the all-time favorite, "kept to themselves"?

Happy faces to the public, nightmare existence

behind the scenes. That was the stuff history was made of.

Murderers like Kelly Proctor.

The more she delved into real-life mysteries, real-life haunting, the more cynical she grew about human nature, secrets and the dreaded idea of love.

She hadn't always been quite so bitter. She had started off life wanting to be open-minded, with an open heart as well. In kindergarten, she clung to the idea of happily ever after. But it was only a few short years afterward that she learned about reality. What men were really like. What she was really like. The cruel darkness of the human condition.

Like Jimmy McMurry back in ninth grade.

She thought he was the greatest. He was tall and handsome and had a quirky sense of irony that amused her. They were science lab partners and had been put together in a couple of other classes for group projects. She had known Jimmy since fifth grade. They had gone through two different schools together, and she figured their bond was strong.

After school one day, Jimmy walked her to the bus stop and asked her if she wanted to go to the park after dinner. Madeline had agreed. It would be fun to be out and about with a guy. They had hung out and had a good time, talking about school, life, movies and swinging on the swings.

They made a habit of meeting several times a week after homework and chores were done. At first, the meetings were harmless. They sat at the park on the swings gossiping about their fellow classmates, lamenting over their marks and worrying about their futures. They had a lot in common, or so Madeline had thought at the time. They liked the same foods, they saw the same movies—sometimes even together—and both thought the principal of the high school was an arrogant asshole.

It wasn't long, maybe a few weeks after they started hanging out in the park, when Jimmy made his move on Madeline. The minute he slung his arm around her in his nervous, twitchy fashion, she knew right then and there what he was up to. Had all those weeks of hanging out really just been a front for him trying to cop a feel? Or had he suddenly looked at her and realized he found her sexy?

She had rather liked the feel of his arm around her and didn't protest when he clumsily tried to kiss her.

From that moment on, whenever they met at the park, they went into the woods and found a place to make out.

As the weeks went by, they went a little further with their petting. One day, he tried to slip his hands down her jeans. She pushed him away.

"No…I don't think we should do that," she said.

"Why not? I just want to feel you."

"I just don't feel like we should," she said.

His face fell, and he turned grumpily away from her. "I thought you liked me."

"I do like you. I just don't think…I mean, we're not going steady or anything, are we?"

"No."

"I mean, you don't even talk to me at school except in the classes we have together."

Jimmy nodded.

It was true.

In the hallways, when they passed each other and

Madeline said, "Hi," Jimmy pointedly looked the other way. As if he were embarrassed to be seen talking to her. She wasn't cool. She wasn't popular.

And she was beginning to wonder if she was his dirty little secret.

They decided to go their separate ways that night, and she thought that was the end of it. However, the next day, it was apparent that some sort of rumor was going around about her. The other kids whispered and pointed at her when she walked down the hall.

Finally, she managed to get the truth from her friend Maria. They were standing at their lockers, juggling books and tugging out papers.

"What is going on?" she asked as a group of girls catcalled her in passing. There was whispering and an eruption of giggles. Madeline scowled and stared at Maria

"Maria, tell me what you know. It's only fair," she demanded.

Maria stared at her with large, brown eyes wide with speculation and wonder with a bit of fear around the edges. "Well…everyone knows," she said softly. She braced herself for Madeline's response. To her surprise, Madeline only narrowed her eyes in confusion.

"What?" Madeline asked.

"What you did," Maria stammered, fumbling with her locker door as she tried to shut it. One of her books slid from her arms and slammed down to the ground, papers spilling out in a fan around it.

"What was it that I did?" Madeline asked. She kneeled down to help Maria gather up the papers. Students walked along the hallway, oblivious to the girls whispering on the floor.

"You know. You put out." Maria sighed. "And I have to say, I didn't think you were the type." She rose and snatched her papers from Madeline's hands.

Madeline stood up shakily, using the locker for support. "Put out? Me?" She asked incredulously.

"Yes, you."

Madeline's mind raced. Even as a 31-year-old adult, she still felt the pang of dismay and disappointment that had spread through her belly like a parasite. The sensation took hold and clung to her, and she had never been able to shake it.

Jimmy had lied. He had betrayed her.

Her friend had actually betrayed her.

When Madeline was finally able to put her thoughts together enough to speak again, she was trembling.

"I didn't do anything. In fact, I pushed him away when he tried to shove his hand down my pants. I can't believe he used me like that."

"Oh, come on, Madeline. Everyone knows you go to the park with him on a regular basis to make out," Maria said as she straightened the books and papers in her arms.

Madeline grew pale, and she slammed the locker door. She snapped the lock tight and double-checked it. The lock held.

"We necked, sure," Madeline said. "I'm not going to deny it, but who knew? We never saw anyone, or at least very rarely."

Maria stared at her. "You really don't know?"

"What's there to know?"

"We all knew all along. He always told Bobby McFarland in great detail about the stuff you got into. And you know what a big mouth Bobby has…"

Madeline took a deep breath. The gnawing in her stomach grew, and there was a tightening that made her want to vomit.

"So he never liked me." She sighed. "He was using me."

"You really thought he liked you?"

"Yes."

"But he always acted like he didn't know you at school. At least, except when you were paired up in classes for projects. How could you think he liked you?"

Even at that tender age, Madeline had learned that sometimes people didn't understand what she thought. She knew she could never explain to Maria how she felt that she and Jimmy had a special friendship. They were buddies who liked to catch snakes and walk along the railroad tracks, and they were make-out buddies learning how to explore a body of the opposite sex. Wasn't that special?

She realized the horrible truth that day. It wasn't. Nothing was special to anyone. She had been blinded by TV shows and movies that romanticized the kind of friendship they had. The reality was cold and grim. She walked away from Maria and down the hallway and went to English class.

The teasing followed her until graduation. Dating was a nightmare of pushing away drunken guys who thought she was a sure thing. Eventually word got out that she was frigid or a lesbian, and she preferred it that way.

By the time she hit university, she had grown a shell of indifference toward men. Now and again, she'd indulge herself when she had one too many beers, but she was always grateful they never stayed.

In her late twenties, she had met a man who had

changed her life. He was quirky and fun and they shared a wonder about the afterlife together. Their time together was far too short, and within a few months, he was dead.

A car crash with a drunk driver. One minute he was talking to her on his cell phone. The next minute, he was dead.

The pain of losing him tore at her like a knife, opening the old wounds and creating new scars. Instead of sharing her pain with her loved ones, she pushed it down and gained 20 pounds. Madeline closed up again and returned to her revolving bedroom of indifference.

Men were interchangeable. Half of their names, she couldn't recall. The wall was thick and no one could penetrate it. Several had tried but had given up in frustration.

However, the wall was beginning to crumble. A small portion of her watched as her friends Maggie and Natasha had each fallen in love. Those two ladies were as cynical as she was, and they had both managed to find rather decent men within the past couple of months.

She knew that as the planets aligned, this month could be her month to find romance. And she thought she knew where to begin her search.

She turned from the mirror and thought about the night before her. She was going to record a séance at a pretty renowned place, the Sleepyhead Inn, and had to fling into gear.

Still warm from the shower, she scurried around the bedroom, pulling together warm clothes before the February chill took hold.

A lot of local people held séances in the winter in Hermana. Many of the homes were bed and breakfasts and had a thriving tourist industry in the summer. When the snowy New England winters hit, tourists didn't venture out to the seaside town, and the locals could unravel their own secrets in peace.

As Madeline passed by her computer in the living room, she flipped the mouse and clicked on her horoscope for the day.

Keep to your New Year's resolution.

Madeline laughed. Hadn't she just been thinking about that damn gym? No matter, it had been only two weeks since she'd last gone. There had been so much going on. People not only enjoyed having séances, but they wanted the added bonus of recording any paranormal activity. That's where she came in.

She checked her digital tape recorder, her still camera, her video camera and her infrared camera. As always, she threw in two extra packages of batteries for each piece of equipment. These séances had a way of sucking the life out of the cameras, and she always ran out of battery power no matter how many she brought.

Every camera lens was dusted and checked and packed away. She double-checked for her chargers. She found a small box and threw in pens, paper, string, tape and other assorted things that could come in handy at the spur of the moment.

The day passed quickly as she made notes about what she hoped to accomplish and drew up lists about images she wanted to capture. She printed off several pages of charts and graphs so they were ready for her to record anything she might experience.

After eating a piece of leftover pizza and half a pint of Ben and Jerry's Coffee Coffee Buzz Buzz Buzz, Madeline washed up and then pulled on her investigative journalist gear. She wore a warm black turtleneck, black jeans, a large crystal around her neck and crystal drop earrings. Her hands were adorned with a ring on every finger, each holding a different gemstone. Cut and polished amethyst, ruby, garnet, aquamarine and amber sparkled from her hands.

Before she left, she checked her paranormal research group message board. There was some discussion about the house she was investigating that night, The Sleepyhead Inn. It had been written up as one of America's top 50 paranormal houses one year. There was speculation that not only was the house built upon land that had once been a graveyard, but that there were several unexplained deaths there.

The Sleepyhead Inn had been a bed and breakfast for only four years. Before that, it had been passed down in the family and was a private home. Guests often complained about strange noises and frightening visions.

Ghostman888 said he'd been at the house before but was unable to record anything he heard. Vincent78 said he had seen pictures of orbs and ectoplasm on the Internet that others had uploaded but had no idea if they were real.

Madeline read with interest different theories about who was haunting the place and why. Even ideas about the graveyard spirits weren't left untouched, as perhaps parts of bodies had been left behind during the mass exhumation.

Jake75 offered theories of the murderers being

ordinary people driven mad by the ghastly sights and sounds they had witnessed. Madeline stared at Jake's icon.

Jake's profile picture was of a wavy patch of ectoplasm he had shot during a stay at a haunted asylum in Texas. Madeline had been to his website many times to read his ghost-hunting journal and to stare at his pictures.

There were several albums of orbs and creepy buildings, but the album she enjoyed the most contained pictures of Jake at conventions, book signings and parties. His deep blue eyes stared intensely into the camera under locks of thick, curly, black hair. He almost always was deeply tanned, as he lived in California and spent a lot of time at haunted lighthouses by night and beaches by day. He often talked about surfing and hoped to one day go on a deep-sea dive to an abandoned wreck.

She wondered what he was like in real life.

Sometimes she would lie awake at night and think about Jake's pictures. She imagined his arms wrapped around her, his lips pressed against hers as he thrust into her. The idea of it inevitably ended with her rubbing her hand against her pussy. She could almost feel the ripples of his muscles along his back as he pumped into her. Always when she came, she remembered he was just a picture on her computer. She would never meet him in real life. He lived somewhere along the coast in California, and she was here in Hermana, on the opposite side of the continent.

But maybe she could change that.

As she gathered her equipment together, she thought about inviting him and some of the others

213

from the online group to help her capture activity at the Kelly Proctor house when she went there in a couple of days. She had mentioned it a few times, and there was always interest in the place on her mailing list. Maybe she should formally extend an invitation and see if anyone would bite.

She buttoned up her coat and smiled.

That would be exactly what she would do.

Imagine if she created a team of investigators that went to haunted houses all across North America. They could shoot documentaries of their expeditions and put them on YouTube. She could write books about their adventures, even self-publish books about her adventures, and give up her freelance work.

Dreaming was always nice, but there was work to be done. Madeline piled up her belongings by the door and double-checked that she had everything. It was very likely she was forgetting something.

She paused as she stared at her gear. Then she remembered. Her purse.

She chuckled as she went to retrieve her large, heavy canvas bag from the couch. It never failed. There was always something.

As she locked the door, she hoped she had remembered everything.

About the Author

Sèphera Girón is the author of 25 books, both fiction and nonfiction, as well as a certified astrologer, tarot reader and numerologist.

She was born in New Orleans and lived just a few doors down from Lee Harvey Oswald for a few months. The Giróns ultimately landed in London Ontario where Sèphera grew up until she left for Toronto to attend York University where she received her B.A, got married, birthed a couple of sons, got divorced, and launched her writing career.

Sèphera's 25 published books under various names span the horror and romance genres, as well as the metaphysical. Sèphera wrote four books with Leisure Horror: *House of Pain, The Birds and the Bees, Borrowed Flesh* and *Mistress of the Dark.* Sèphera's work with Samhain Horror includes *Captured Souls, Flesh Failure, Experiments in Terror* and *A Penny Saved.* She is currently working on the erotic romance/horror 12-part *Witch Upon a Star* series featuring astrological signs and witchcraft.

Sèphera received her certificate in Tarot, Numerology, and Astrology from the School of Metaphysical Sciences International. She also has Reiki and Touch for Health certificates. She currently writes a weekly astrological column for RomanceBeat.com.

Sèphera reads tarot and also enjoys going to haunted houses. She's stayed overnight at the Lizzie Borden House six times, twice at a haunted mansion in California, and recently attended a Writers Retreat at the Stanley Hotel in Colorado.

Sèphera lives in Toronto by the lake where she works as a freelance writer, freelance editor, and tarot reader. You can follow her on twitter.com/sephera, youtube.com/sephera, instagram.com/sepheragiron, sephwritter666.blogspot.com, tarotpaths.blogspot.com

Other Paranormal Riverdale Avenue Books You Might Enjoy

The Virgin Witch and The Vampire King
By Trinity Blacio

The Virgin Witch and the Vampire King
Book One: Wedding Bells Times Four
By Trinity Blacio

The Virgin Witch and the Vampire King
Book Two: Training a Wife
By Trinity Blacio

Embracing the Winds
By Trinity Blacio

Her Stepbrothers' Demands
By Trinity Blacio

Her Stepbrothers are Aliens
By Trinity Blacio

Her Stepbrothers are Demons
By Trinity Blacio

Her Stepbrothers are Blood Suckers
By Trinity Blacio

Stoned Love
By Trinity Blacio

Possession of the Soul: Book One of The Fantasy
is Alive Series

Made in the USA
Middletown, DE
02 July 2016